BAILING OUT

Published by Honeybee Books
Broadoak, Dorset
www.honeybeebooks.co.uk

Printed in the UK using paper from sustainable sources

ISBN: 978-1-910616-61-1

BAILING OUT

A Novel

Brent Shore

For Heather,
for Ystradgynwyn

One two three four five
Once I caught a fish alive
Six seven eight nine ten
Then I put it back again.

Why did you let it go?
Because it bit my finger so
Which finger did it bite?
This little finger on my right.

Traditional English nursery rhyme

PROLOGUE

COUNTY HOSPITAL, DURNOVER WING

Late July

Just like the day before and the day before that, the air in here today holds the faintly vegetal taste of decay.

The door to the private room has been wedged open on account of the dead heat of the afternoon and through the gap a strip light on the ceiling of the corridor can be seen flickering on and off, on and off, hesitating like a child plucking up the courage to jump a stream, on and off, and finally on. Gabe replays an old image of his son, a year or two ago, leaping across the little gulley he'd dug when they were laying down the pond in the back garden. It isn't just the flickering that bothers Gabe: there's a scratchy hum that comes and goes with it. What remains is a gently irritating monotone.

There is no need for artificial lighting in the private room, for its wide windows allow a flood of natural sunlight to fill it, to glint off the silvery edges of the monitors, off the metal frames of the furniture and the drip-stand, to radiate from the spotless walls, bleaching the crisp bed-sheets with an intensity that hurt his eyes. If he were the kind of person who wore sunglasses indoors he would be wearing a pair right now. But out in the corridor there is far less natural light, or so it would appear. Gabe sees a porter slowly pushing a trolley of laundry past the open doorway, followed by his long wavering shadow. And suddenly the strip light cuts out with a soft buzz, this time for good.

For a little while now there have been four people in the private room. It is not a small room but it feels cramped. The three who are able move from one position to another, from the window to a chair, from the bedside to the trolley, as if in a mechanical dance, brush past each other in near silence, exchanging spaces like pieces on a chessboard. For want of something better to do Gabe is pouring himself a glass of water and is spilling a little on to the plastic tray. His wife Grace is suddenly at the wide windows, peering out, watching the flimsiest of breezes touch the leaves of a young sycamore; she hasn't spoken to him for at least five minutes. Now the nurse is at the door, casting a glance down the corridor, as if she is expecting someone. The fourth person, the only one who doesn't move, who cannot move, of course, is Don: horizontal, fixed in time and space like an Egyptian mummy, legs held rigid, head looped in bandages, eyes shut, mouth clamped, nose pinned by tubing, covered to his chin by layers of sheets, his chest rises and falls but by barely half an inch, the only evidence of a loose hold on life.

Then, trapped in this space with its door wedged open but its wide windows closed, traces of the smell again: neither sweat, nor urine, nor disinfectant, not even a cocktail of all three. Gabe decides it is the stain of stale food, hanging in the reconditioned air like zombie breath.

"That *is* a lovely photograph."

Gabe looks up. The nurse has moved to the bedside table

and, in her rich West African accent, is speaking to him, to Grace, to them both.

"This one," she says, her dark plump face creasing into a smile. She straightens the photo, standing it up against a box of tissues. "You look like the perfect family, yes, you really do."

It is a simple enough family group, posed and caught in the sunshine by an amateur or even a self-timer: five happy faces, three generations in colourful holiday clothes standing together for a few seconds in what looks like a private garden or a small park. Juliet recognises the younger man on the right as her patient's son, nervous, edgy, hovering around the bed like a shy man on the fringes of a party. There to the left of the picture is his wife, looking trim and pretty, lovely blonde curls, smiling for the camera, very self-aware; and here she is now, still staring out of the window, bored, much shorter hair with new highlights, and has she put on a little weight in the meantime? But at the centre of the photograph are an older couple. It's clearly their day. The man is around fifty, she guesses, healthy, good complexion, he looks confident, alert. His hair is short and thick, a greyer version of his son's. But Juliet has never seen his full face for real, concealed as it now is in heavy dressings, by the oxygen mask, the intrusive tubing. The other woman in the picture is standing very close to him, one arm behind his back perhaps, hugging him to her. She too looks contented, maybe a little tired, her sharp, intelligent features captured in a moment of celebration. Don has been lying in this hospital bed for three days, but, as far as the nurse knows, this woman has never set foot in the place. In front of them both is the child: a very young boy with an eager, spirited energy about him and a smile that radiates his pride in being part of this special group.

3

"Yes, perfect," says Gabe with a tight laugh, and Juliet cannot fail to catch its undisguised irony.

"I think it's pretty good of all of us," he goes on quietly. "Quite a rarity, really. Mum was never happy with how she looked in photos. There are plenty of pictures of Dad and me: on holiday, posing in the garden with a cricket bat, you know. But Mum..."

"I haven't met your mother. You know, visiting Don here on the ward."

"No, you won't have. I thought you knew. My mother died about a year ago. An accident."

"Oh. I'm sorry. I'd no idea, Mr Percey. I thought perhaps...

"Stupid really. The most stupid accident."

Suddenly Grace, who is now crouching by the open bed-side cupboard, interrupts:

"Didn't you bring your dad some shirts? I can't see any in here. Gabe, are you listening?

"Sorry, er, I thought I did. Isn't there a tee-shirt in there somewhere?"

"I can't see one."

"Right at the back?"

"I am looking right at the back. There is no tee-shirt, no shirt in here at all, at the front or right at the back."

"I must have left it at home. Anyway, he won't need any of his own clothes yet. I'll bring them in next time."

"You're getting so forgetful these days..."

"I have got quite a lot on my mind, Grace."

The nurse cuts in:

"Anyway, it *is* a lovely photograph."

She is checking the monitors and writing numbers on to charts on a pink clipboard.

Gabe moves back over to the plastic-backed chair by his father's bed and sits down to take the weight off his feet. He picks up the photo and looks at it for a moment or two.

"I thought, you know, when he wakes up..."

Grace pushes hard at the little cupboard door until it shuts with a click.

"*If* he wakes up," she suggests.

"*When* he wakes up, it would be the first thing he sees. If we're not here. He'd see the picture and maybe he'd recognise a face. Help him regain a sense of who he is. Where he is. I don't know, it's just a thought. Something familiar, something to stimulate a reaction..."

"It's a lovely idea," offers Juliet.

Gabe says nothing more.

"What's your little boy's name?"

"Sorry?"

"The little one in the photograph, what's his name?"

"Oliver. That's Oliver. He's seven. He was four or five in this photo. He wouldn't stand still."

In three days the nurse hasn't seen Gabe properly smile until now.

"It was a party for my Mum and Dad's thirtieth wedding anniversary. A ruby wedding bash in the back garden; just family and a few old friends."

Grace, listening:

"Pearl, not ruby. Ruby's the fortieth."

Gabe looks across the room at his wife. She is standing by the window once again, staring out at the cloudless sky, her back to him. He looks back at the photograph.

"Ollie couldn't understand how his grandparents could be married for so long. He could just about count that far."

Another smile, a little shallower.

"Thirty years. And now it's all fallen apart, hasn't it?"

"Oh, be optimistic. Please, Mr Percey. You must. Really you must. Your father has made very good progress. His internal organs are all sound. The bleeding has stopped. He really is on the mend. The doctors are confident he will come out of this very soon and will make a good recovery. A proper recovery. Please..."

Grace, bored with the view, has turned her back to the window. She sighs gently, casting a look towards the bandaged patient, the tubes and the drips, the oxygen, the splints, the soft, regular patterns on the monitors. His sleeping eyes. He looks so helpless, chest lifting and sinking in a slow, shallow rhythm like a tiring metronome set to *adagio*. So vulnerable. She sees her husband's ruddy face. Poor Gabe. Her husband is doing his level best to be supportive, of course he is, and it's not such an effort: selflessness comes quite naturally to him. But that's Gabriel: loyal and steadfast. Gabe the rock. Rock solid. Which is all very well, but sometimes she wishes he were a rock that rolled just a little more.

His moist eyes meet hers.

"You look lovely in this, Grace," he says, still transfixed by the photo. "Blue suits you, I've always said that, haven't I?"

"We should go." She is not in the mood for flattery. "It's after four."

The nurse places the pink clipboard into a transparent pouch attached to the foot of the bed.

"I'm leaving you now," she says. "Other patients to see to. I'm just down the corridor if you need me. It was nice to see you again, Mr Percey, Mrs Percey. Stay as long as you like. I'll see you next time if I'm on, perhaps."

"We're leaving too," says Grace, picking up a newspaper lying at the foot of the bed, folding it briskly and tucking it between the straps of her bag. "Gabe, we should go. We need to pick up Oliver and then..."

"Yes, I did hear you the first time."

Gabe returns the photograph to its place on the bedside table. Standing up, he runs his fingers through his hair and then takes hold of his father's limp right hand. He looks hard at the closed eyes, the tubes clamped around the fleshy nose, the bandages framing the jaw, set to silent.

"I'll be back again tomorrow, Dad. Tomorrow. Stay strong, old man."

ONE

The lake-dwellers had wanted to construct a geometrically perfect steel-framed cube but it seemed that they had been given only a motley collection of damaged materials.

And so, at the very bottom of the lake, set flat against the sand and barely visible in the faint shafts of sunlight that refract through the watery depths, here beyond the shelf-line, is the cage: a space the size of a small room enclosed by an irregular box-like structure of hastily connected scaffolding poles.

Sensing movement inside it, Don is peering into the space, squinting between the cold, rusty bars. Quite at ease, he swims around the side to get a better view. He is breathing as effortlessly underwater, down here in the depths of this lake, as he would be standing on the shore.

The thin light is playful, casting moving shadows and then just as suddenly revealing a line, a new shape in the liquid gloom. As a shimmering ray illuminates his target, he now sees the prisoner clearly before him. It is a woman, sitting, unconcerned by her captivity, at an empty writing desk. A small shoal of minnows skitter by its narrow carved legs. The woman is reading from a single sheet of paper which is wafted gently by the currents in a slow rhythm with her long fine hair and the soft folds of her nightdress.

Anxiously, Don is pressing his face between the poles.

"Carole...," he calls, and hears his voice carry through the water. "Carole, look, it's me!"

Agitated, Don is pulling at the bars of the makeshift cage, but the woman does not hear him. She does not turn her head towards him. She is absorbed in her task, whatever it may be.

The bars are loose; they rattle but they will not yield.

"Carole!"

He is shouting louder now, and as he twists away to swim to the far side of the cage, he suddenly realises that his wrist is trapped at an angle where upright and transom cross.

Now Don is tugging his hand away. He is still caught, like a fish on a line.

The woman is still reading.

Lazily the light changes and only the shadowy outlines remain. In the next shaft of iridescence he can see that his wrist, his right wrist, is now clamped to a vertical tube of scaffolding by a pair of handcuffs: silver, glinting in the faltering beams. He tugs again, panicking now, as hard as he can, but the cuffs are locked tight and he is snared.

Don is pulling back and forth, and the frame of the cage is rocking at its base, casting up eddies of sand from the lake bed.

"Carole!" he screams, but the woman cannot feel the cage shaking. Her eyes are set fast on the printed page in her delicate hands.

Then, as the faint sunrays alter again, the waters on the far side of the cage appear briefly aglow and Don recognises another shape swimming towards it. Out of the shadows emerges the figure of Neptune, god of springs and lakes and rivers, Roman god of the sea, naked, bearded, and now aiming the glinting prongs of a trident towards the cage.

Don's eyes meet the creature's through the shimmering patterns of light. He sees sparks of fire in them.

The cage is still between them. Once more Don tugs vainly against the handcuffs. Neptune strikes his trident hard against the bars of the cage: a metallic ratatat-tat distorted by the water. The minnows scatter like a firework exploding. The woman looks up, suddenly disturbed, and smiles serenely.

But Don is now beside himself.

"Carole!" he pleads, as Neptune turns and starts to swim smoothly around the cage towards him.

Don jerks his hand away from the bar, hopelessly. But this time, somehow, he is free; the cuffs have opened and frantically he turns away and flees, kicking his legs hard against the water. With all the power he can muster he stretches his arms out ahead of him, pulls them back through the mass, again and again, to lurch away and upwards, quickly upwards, towards the sunlight flickering above on the surface of the lake.

COUNTY HOSPITAL

August

My name is Donald Percey and at least I can remember that much. When you wake up from a long, troubled sleep in a cold, dark place you need a few straws to grab hold of. Well, I never forgot who I am. And I knew I was in a hospital bed, in a brightly lit room. On my own, I thought. And I knew that, for all the pain, I was alive. I don't know how close I was to dying but the first doctor I saw here had the expression on his face of a man who was about to defuse a live bomb.

The very first thing I remember was listening to a woman's voice telling me her name. A name I didn't recognise: Juliet. Of course I can remember it now. She said she'd been talking to me for days. She had a pretty voice, chirrupy and clear, and she told me she had come from Africa to nurse me back to life. The delicate features of her round open face came gently into focus before my blinking eyes. The light hurt and she moved to a window and pulled down a blind. She told me where I was and asked me if I knew who I was. It seemed like a daft question; of course I knew who I was: Don Percey, aged fifty-four. I think I wanted to tell her I was a detective, but as speech was impossible no words came out, which was disconcerting. In any case that would have been wrong, of course. I haven't been in the force for eighteen months. But I'm pretty sure I would have got my name right.

She told me she was going to fetch a doctor, but before she left the room she reached over for a square of card lying close to my bed. Juliet smiled and handed it to me. This was mine, she said - a picture of the people who loved me. *Don't go away, now*, she ordered; it was her little joke, I suppose.

My head was held rigidly in some sort of brace. I had sensation and freedom in my right arm and with a little effort I held the card up to my eye line and focused my fragile sight on a familiar photograph. One that I recognised from a frame at home: a family portrait of the not-so-extensive Perceys. It was a happy moment, frozen in a lens: all eyes forwards, some toothy smiles, some closed, contented grins. Arms around shoulders and waists, my left hand gently resting on little Oliver's curly brown hair. In my right, what looked like a glass of wine. Carole had one too, slightly raised and her wide mouth half open in a "cheers", her lively hazel eyes looking so slightly above the camera. To either side of us, our son Gabriel, looking every inch the fitter, younger, taller version of his dad, and his wife Grace, tanned and relaxed in a powder-blue man's shirt.

It's been two weeks since I woke up. That's what the nurse says. And Gabe too, who's been in to see me every day. I think. Gabe is my son. His wife's name is Grace. I have already mentioned that. She doesn't always come with him. That's okay, though. She's a busy woman. She runs a shop, I think. Or she used to.

It seems I was attacked by some madman.

I don't remember any attack, but I've been told that I was found unconscious in a bus depot by a dog-walker and I hadn't just tripped over an oil drum. He spotted a cab light still on in the dark, the driver's door still ajar. I've been left with a pair of broken legs, three cracked ribs, massive bruising, a fractured skull and a broken jaw. Quite a tally.

So I have to try to remember. There's a copper I recognise who asks me questions all the time, when the nurses let him. I can only nod as my jaw is set. I do get tired easily, even now. And headaches. Awful headaches. As I'm staying awake a little longer each day, they've given me this laptop. I'm to write down my thoughts and recollections in my lucid moments. *Take it from the beginning*, somebody said. *Take it from wherever you like*, someone else chipped in. *Extrapolate. Be creative. If it's a bit disjointed, don't worry, we'll work it out. Give us detail. Let us worry about making sense of it.*

They want a statement.

Fragments of your memory, Don, somebody said. *As much or as little as you can. Scraps of facts. Little descriptions that come to mind. Any of it could be valuable.*

Even dreams? asked a doctor who looked no older than a teenager.

Especially dreams, somebody said.

It's a kind of therapy, I suppose. The doctors agree that if I could help the police and help myself at the same time, reconnecting the circuits, reordering the files, as it were, then everyone's a winner.

It's a nice new laptop.

But I do get tired.

Writing's never been a problem, and I want to help. I was a police officer myself. I had to write report after report, of course. I tidied up witness statements. I used to proofread my boss's annual development plan and then translate it from *Coppingese* into something more convincing as readable English. Some complained about the paperwork. Not me. I was quite at home with a piece of prose to compose.

I made Detective Sergeant. Not a high-flyer. Steady though.

I've written enough for today.

I'm feeling okay in my head this afternoon. No pain yet.

What the hell am I doing here in hospital? I need to answer

that question. They say I was attacked. Brutally attacked - so I must have deserved it. Not a random attack. Somebody lying in wait for me, following me, knowing my routine. What have I done to deserve an attempt on my life like that? Was it someone from my past as a copper? I left the force over two years ago. I think I already said that. Nobody leaves with pats on the back from all the jacks you've worked with - you always tread on a few toes -but as things go I thought I'd got away clean and clear. A few minor gripes and grudges, but no festering wounds. And as for the villains, they're either insignificant, infirm or inside. And anyway, I was a minor player. Maybe I'm wrong but I don't think I left that much of an impression. I was never the action hero with a jackhammer drive to clean up the county. Not like Coppinger. I had no vindictive streak. I never made it personal.

But somebody else did.

Somebody made it extremely personal.

I need to think beyond the police force. Take my thinking to the very recent past. I've a statement to write, but where do I start? The cast of characters is vague and the sequence of events is mistier still.

I can see faces but some names have gone. At least for now.

My wife was Carole. Carole's dead. She must be. One way or another she has left me. So, has she left me, or left me behind? She hasn't been to see me and I think she would have done if she'd wanted to or been able to. Gabriel's been a lot. He came again last night.

I see a small round-faced boy. I have a grandson, I'm sure but he's not the boy I see. Gabe's son is Oliver. Oliver is much younger than the boy I see. And this boy's a scamp.

And Geena. Geena Dale. I need to remember her. She's at the heart of it. She must be. I do remember her spiky red hair and her crazy, scatty smile. Full of mischief. How did our paths cross?

Cherchez la femme, as they used to say.

Is Geena Dale the reason I'm lying here with broken bones and fits of nausea? *Cherchez la femme*. A detective's default setting. That or *Follow the money*.

I can't think about this any more today.

This typing is taking longer than I thought. It's a slow old job and I've got a headache coming on again.

TWO

The scene plays in a minibus. A woman's voice fades in: an elderly, smoky voice, a voice of experience and wisdom, yet a voice of lightness, of humour and of a tangible warmth.

Rita is rambling, on a verbal downhill roll, but Don doesn't mind; he has trouble talking and driving at the same time, but *listening* and driving is not such a problem.

"Polo's mum is a bit of a one-off," she is saying. "She's nice, really, but I do feel sorry for her. All those kids, no steady father for them to speak of. She does make an effort, at least she does most of the time, but she's not the most reliable. *Flaky*, my husband would call her. That's his word for anyone in his team who doesn't show up at the pub when there's a darts match on. *Flaky*. Well, that's one word he might use! There are others, if you catch my meanin', Don."

She chuckles to herself, takes a quick half-breath and rolls on:

"She'll never ring me to tell me Polo's not comin' to school, he's ill or runnin' late or whatever. They're supposed to let us know, the parents. She says she's lost my number. I've lost count of how many times I've wrote it down for her. Next she'll say she can't find her phone. If we have to go down there for no reason, if he's not comin' to school, then it's a detour for nothin.'"

"It would save us, what, ten minutes if we missed out his village?" Don asks, to himself as much as to his passenger. He is concentrating perhaps a little harder than usual this morning, responsible not only for his passengers (six children, did she say?) but also for someone else's vehicle. And a sluggish brute of a vehicle at that, steering through the morning traffic like a drunk on a dance floor.

"We could stick with the main road or even go by Victoria Bridge. Does he miss school often, what's his name, Polo?"

He catches the top of her head in the rear-view mirror, her fluffy, unruly grey hair, then the lines on her narrow forehead, but not quite her eyes, which is disconcerting.

"Now and then," says Rita. "He does get lots of coughs, you know, chesty ones, but most of the time, I think, he just can't be bothered. Can't be bothered with it, you know. He's lazy. Don't like school much, I reckon that's the top and bottom of it. He pulls the wool over his mum's eyes."

"Can't she insist that he gets up and gets himself ready for the bus on time?"

"I don't think she's got the stomach for a fight some mornin's. And anyway, she's not always up herself. Some mornin's we get round there and there'll be no sign of life at eight o'clock. No sign of life at all. All the curtains closed, and four or five of them inside fast asleep."

Don has stopped for a knot of traffic at a red light. He turns to face Rita, but she's looking down, rummaging for something in her bag.

"What's he on our bus for?" he asks. "What's *his* problem with language?"

"There's nothin' wrong with his talkin'. No, by rights he should go to the local school in their village - at least until he's eleven."

Rita looks up and smiles a shallow smile of resignation.

"The lights have changed, Don, by the way."

Don shuffles round on his seat, back to face the road, to cradle the big ugly steering wheel in his hands.

"But they can't cope with him," she goes on. "And they've tried him at two others, I think. He skipped it so often he was gettin' left behind. So he goes to the Special Unit because they can offer small classes. He's such a handful. At least he was backalong. I think he's gettin' better. He's ten now. He's had all sorts of problems. Mainly fightin' other children. *Anger management*. Isn't that the latest phrase? He's had issues with his teachers: swearin', hittin' out, that kind of thing. Don't worry, Don, he can be as sweet as a lamb on the bus."

And just here the smoky voice starts to fade out.

"If he likes you."

*

The same scene, a little later. Two small children have joined the bus. Over the grumbly drone of the old diesel engine, Rita's voice plays again:

"He's lovely with these little ones, when he's in the mood. You like Polo, don't you, Reece? Reece, you like having Polo sat next to you, don't you?"

Even perched on booster seats, some of the children are hidden from Don's view. In time he will recognise their faltering, shrill little voices, he will be able to distinguish their silences, their hesitations, their stammers and stumbles, one from another.

"Polo's nice," says Reece, after a moment. "He gives me choc... chockilit."

"Yes, well, he shouldn't really be having chocolate on the bus," suggests Rita, "should he?"

"Not on the bus," says Reece, who understands Rita's rules

perfectly well. "At school. At school at playtime. He gives me choc... chockilit."

"I didn't think he played with the younger ones," she offers, back to Don. "He didn't used to be allowed to play with them. There was a time when he was supervised one to one at break-times."

Suddenly another squeaky voice sings out from the seats at the rear: it is a little girl whose seat belt still needs attention from Rita.

"I don't like Polo," she trills. "He wunned into me. He knocked me. Knocked me down. And Jessie. He wunned into Jessie, he did."

Rita, finally clicking the child's buckle secure:

"Well, I expect he can be a bit rough, Emily. I shouldn't think he'd run into you in purpose, though, would he?"

"He knocked me down."

"Did you tell a teacher?"

"And Jessie. She telled, she did," she answers, nodding for emphasis.

"It's here, on the left, Don," says the PA. "It's a bit awkward to turn round at the bottom, but there's usually enough space if the neighbours have tidied up a bit. Otherwise you'll have to reverse out."

Don tuts, flicks on the indicator, slows the minibus to a crawl and turns sharply into the lane leading down to The Pavilions.

*

The same scene, a little later still. Rita, sliding the rickety door shut, makes a theatrical point of formal introductions:

"This is, Don, Polo. Our new driver. Say hello."

Don has turned to greet the newcomer or at the very least, to offer eye contact and a smile. The boy, the oldest child on the bus, makes a performance of finding a seat that suits him this morning but says nothing.

"Morning, Polo," shouts Don down the bus. "How are you today?"

No response. The boy is looking out of the window, back towards his house, back towards the streaky red paintwork of his mother's front door.

"Where's your mum?" asks Rita. "She usually sees you to the bus and has a word."

"She's in a mood," mumbles the boy.

"In a mood?"

"She's indoors with Tiffany. She spilled her breakfast on the floor. She went off on one."

"Never mind. Has she made you somethin' for your lunch-box?"

"She give me a bag of crisps and says to wait outside for you."

"Right. Okay. Well, well done for being on time, Polo."

The boy grumbles something else but Don is already reversing the vehicle into a narrow pathway by the side of the houses, trying to avoid driving over a scruffy patch of lawn. Another infant voice is lifted over the coughing of the engine: it sounds like Reece:

"I like crips. Rita, I like crips. Do you?"

I had the dream again, the recurring one, the one where I'm underwater, the one with Carole sitting at the bottom of a lake in a cage. This time I swam right to the surface and emerged, gasping for air, blinking my eyes to clear the water from them. I could taste salt. I can still taste it now, weirdly, as I tap out these words. I was in the open sea, not a lake at all. Well, almost: a kind of wide inlet, the mouth of a river whose sheer stony banks I could see in the distance. I could hear voices, the voices of children: children I didn't know. I had surfaced in the middle of some kind of sailing academy, surrounded by the splashing hulls of little dinghies toing and froing in the sunlight, their dazzling white sails filled with a steady, warm wind.

Dreams? Especially dreams? I'm not sure how much help that will be to anyone trying to understand why I'm in this state.

I try to remember the assault on me but find it simpler not to try at all and just let the memories drift in and out, which they have started to do, randomly, short and yet sharp, but distant, nothing from as recent as July. It is easier to remember what happened months ago, even years ago, than it is to recall the details of the attack. The days leading up to it are a blur, a series of gaps.

After years of debilitating duties on the force, and a few empty months after retiring, the first day in a new job provided an excitement and a clarity of thought that is harder to erase.

I spent two years in the early part of my police career in the traffic section. I passed as an Advanced Driver without a second's hesitation and was allowed to pilot cars on and off road, ride big bikes, drive trucks and vans, some fast and others even faster. I was encouraged to put in for a PCV licence at that time. Years ago. I thought I'd add another string to my bow, which it was, I suppose, but I never had cause to use it. Well, not until last September.

It had crossed my mind to do some volunteering work with old folks' groups or youth groups, or offering to drive a minibus for a care home or a hospital. Taking parties out for days at the seaside, adventure playgrounds, or to gardens somewhere. It was all very vague but I had mentioned it briefly to Gabe. Then I saw the advert for a part-time mini-bus driver, a private company called Pattermore's - school runs, county council contract - and I thought, that'll keep me occupied: a nice easy job, tootling around, stop me thinking about getting old without Carole. I didn't stop to consider how I'd deal with boisterous children, moody teenagers up to no good, answering back, littering the seats, but then I didn't have to. The job I was offered, shuttling six prima-ry-age children (six!) to a special Speech & Language Unit out of town came with its own PA. I'd never had a PA before. Detective Sergeants don't merit one. Actually she was what is known as a Passenger Assistant, and that's how I met Rita. Her house was the first pick-up, of course, and the last drop-off. First thing every morning interpretations of the weather forecast and last thing every afternoon shared thoughts on tea and television. She sat with the children, kept them calm, chatted and sang silly songs with them, wiped their noses, stopped them arguing, and ferried them across the car park into classes like a mother hen in her reflective daf-fodil-yellow gilet with its county council logo.

There wasn't much arguing. Most of them had severe dif-ficulty with coherent speech and conversation was short, snappy, often funny. They enjoyed looking out for tractors or being the first one to spot a pheasant. Rita was brilliant with them. All of them were younger than eight and were sweet-natured. With the exception, that is, of Polo Dale who was older, ten or eleven, I think, and much less predictable.

Polo or Paulo? I misheard Rita at first. I checked my passenger list: Polo. Polo? Were his parents mint lovers? Were they inspired by a thirteenth-century Venetian explorer? Unlikely. Neither could I imagine Geena Dale at ease in the refined company of the sporty equestrian set on the grander estates in the north-east of the county. Was there a Polish angle? Did the boy have a Pole for a father? Apparently not, but I do remember someone else who did. Rita, as usual, had the inside track. Over the years she had got to know the mother pretty well. At her wits' end and with no responsible adult in the home to turn to, Geena Dale had confided many secrets to Rita, one of which was that, following the fashion of naming a child after the place of its conception, she admitted that Polo was the fruit of a cramped, sweaty union up a dark farm-track on the back seat of a small Volkswagen.

Almost without exception, the many villages of the county present a face to the visitor of pride, prosperity and a little smugness. Tidy, pretty and self-assured, they offer a glimpse of an idyllic escape from ugliness and brutality: here the jaded outsider from the city will discover the cosy pub, the leafy churchyard and the dinky school. They will be reassured by plump thatch, birdsong and soft sunlit gardens; they will be enchanted by high-hedged secret bridle-ways, grassy slopes ripe with sheep, the damp tang from a stable-yard or the sweet scent of wood-smoke in the winter. Hidden away at each village's edge, however, out by a faded business park, or in the shadows of a disused railway arch, or perhaps down by a water treatment plant, is a small estate of social housing: a quota-filling concession to help accommodate the rural poor.

In Polo Dale's village the provision was limited, as far as I know, to only one row of five draughty homes: The Pavilions. There is nothing ornamental about them, no frivolous decorative effect to soften the blunt, functional aspect of the 1960s-built terrace of council houses, forced into a narrow plot of uneven land which slopes down to a litter-strewn, brook-side pathway. I knew it, having been witness to at least one drugs raid in my probationary days on the force, and having visited several temporary residents on the merry-go-round of occupancy with more recent inquiries over stolen property. Always at No.5, if I remember rightly.

The first time Rita directed me to No.1 The Pavilions, I was surprised to see a boy, alone, waiting on the step outside the front door: an apple-shaped face held flint-grey eyes which stared hard at me, piercing the windscreen in their intense curiosity. A tight-fitting royal blue school jumper barely disguised an ample amount of puppy fat. Rita said that even before the summer holidays he'd been anxious to know who the new bus driver would be. He was already at the door of the vehicle before I had pulled over to make a proper stop. There was no sign of his mother on my first morning at their house.

I remember we didn't get off to the best of starts, Polo and me, but then who expects conversational fireworks at eight o'clock on a grey Monday morning between a ten-year-old child who's been out of bed for less than fifteen minutes and a middle-aged stranger with a dopey grin? I didn't see Polo for most of the journey to school. He was bobbing about on a seat two or three rows back and out of the eye line of my rear-view mirror. But from the moment he stepped into the bus I could smell him. On the first day of a brand new term, when a couple of the other children had on fresh new uniforms and even their back-packs smelled of plasticky newness, Polo carried with him a smell I recognised: the lingering mix of unwashed clothes and domestic animals, of stale tobacco and slapdash hygiene. Around the boy hung the clawing stink of poverty.

THREE

The scene plays in a police station; in the familiar glass-panelled office of Detective Inspector Edmund Coppinger to be more precise. It is one of those dark days of autumn when the lights are on inside in the middle of the morning and outside the warm rain is lashing the pavements and flooding the gutters. Sitting behind his desk, top button undone, rugby club tie askew, Coppinger is opening and closing his mouth. He is thick-set, more than a little overweight, and his voice, curiously more tenor than *basso profundo*, has reached audible volume.

"Ah, DS Percey," he starts. "Come in, come in. At last. We've started without you, as you can see."

Don has noticed a third figure in the office, a slight, athletic man in a coffee-coloured suit standing at ease in the space between desk and door.

"This is DS Tufts," the DI picks up. "DS Paul Tufts, on secondment from the Met, as you know."

Don and Tufts are already on the point of shaking hands.

"Don Percey. Good to have you on board, as they say." It's a feeble line and Don is already regretting the cliché.

"Thanks," says the younger man, straight-faced.

Coppinger invites neither man to sit in the one available seat in the room, leaving them both to stand self-consciously while he stretches back into his padded swivel chair.

"DS Tufts is here for twelve months, in the first instance. Come to have a sniff around the county. Come to get some fresh country air into his lungs. Been in the city too long, have we, Tufts?"

"Well, not exactly, sir. I am a city boy at heart, I suppose, but as you know, my superiors thought it'd be a good idea to have a change of scene, a change of environment."

"Get you out of your comfort zone?"

"Something like that, sir."

"Anyway, where've you been, Donny boy? We've had to start without you. Can't keep a busy man from the Met waiting forever." A wink to Tufts.

Percey coughs to clear his throat.

"Sorry, sir. I've been on the phone with the headman at the YOI. Bit longer than I expected."

"You've been bending his ear about Kermit?"

"Kermit, yes, and others. He wanted a word about Evergreen. You remember, the lad who was done for the arson attacks."

"Really."

Addressing Tufts directly, Coppinger makes as if to apologise:

"DS Percey has an obsession with Kermit..."

Tufts declines to ask for an explanation, knowing that one is coming in any case.

"Ain't that right, Donny?"

"Well, not exactly. I wouldn't call it an obsession." And to Tufts:

"He's someone I've been trying to get to do a little more for our benefit. And for his too in the long run."

"He's an informer?"

"A grass who doesn't really grass, eh, Donny?" interrupts Coppinger. "We're not exactly sure he's worth all the time and the trouble though, are we, in all honesty? Strictly small-time, low-life stuff. He's not going to unlock the door to the crown jewels for us, is he?"

This time Don doesn't answer. He's not going to let the man wind him up this morning. Not in front of a new boy.

"The crown jewels?" asks Tufts after a pause.

"He won't lead us to the major players in the area," says Coppinger, fighting a yawn. Was last night a late one? "The ones we want to break. The higher-end suppliers, drugs, vice, fraud. It's not just sheep-rustling and cider-fuelled domestics down here in the sticks, Sergeant."

"I didn't for one moment think..."

"No, I'm sure you didn't, bright boy like you."

Don notices that the rain has stopped beating on the windows.

Tufts is talking again: "So you have what you might call a Mr Big, or several, pulling the strings locally?"

Don tries to stifle a laugh.

"DS Percey is right to smile," says the DI. "This isn't Chicago. We don't really do *Mr Bigs*. But we do have a few *Mr Slightly Larger Than Averages*. Some more obvious than others. Some lazy bastards. Some more cunning. Some more ambitious. Some come and go, just passing through. Slippery as eels."

"Laurie Somers, for example," offers Don.

Tufts is about to say something but he hesitates. The

moment passes. Coppinger sits up in his chair, fixes Tufts with a stare and ploughs on:

"He's one on the radar at the moment, that's true. Mr Somers. Laughing boy Lawrence. Larry the Leery. He runs the family business: electricals. Clever bastard. You must read the files, DS Tufts. In fact, you have been allowed access to everything we have here, apparently. Permission from those in heaven. Even DS Percey's fucking shopping lists. You can trawl through it all."

Tufts smiles at Percey. You do well to tolerate him, his eyes are saying. Coppinger has turned to look out of the window.

"Thank God it's finally stopped pissing down," he says to nobody in particular.

"Tell me a bit more about Kermit, then, please, Don," says Tufts. "I can call you Don, can I?"

"Yes, of course. Of course you can. Most people do."

"And Paul, please."

His tone is earnest, his accent is nondescript, blandly southern with no identifying edges: classless, educated, neutral. And softly spoken; his voice is easier on the ear than Coppinger's bark.

"Kermit's one of many lost souls in town," Don begins. "And there are plenty like him in the villages. Left school at fifteen, unemployed, no family to speak of..."

"Kermit, that's not his real name, right?"

"Everyone calls him that," says Don, smiling. "Ever since he was a kid, it seems. His real name is Tommy Kremitz. It's not far to get from there to Kermit, especially when you are six-year-old with big eyes, skinny legs and a goofy wide mouth.

"And a squeaky fucking annoying voice," adds Coppinger, eyes still on the road two floors below.

"He is one of life's victims," Don goes on. "Bullied mercilessly all through school, but he always bounced back, maybe diminished, and found a way to survive the treatment."

He hands across a document wallet, and continues:

"Here's his file. There's plenty in it as you can see. Take a look, if you're interested. He's been up to no good since he was thirteen, thinking crime was the way to impress his peers. Petty theft, selling on stolen cigarettes, then cannabis; burglary, farm buildings, garden sheds..."

Coppinger has heard it all before. He picks up a newspaper and begins to read it absent-mindedly. Meanwhile Don has more for Tufts:

"His father's an interesting one. He might have even come on your radar. He moved back to Hammersmith when Kermit was five. He left him behind with his mother. I think they *were* actually married."

"Name?"

"Tadeusz Kremitz. He came to the UK in 1990; one of the first wave after the whole Solidarity thing broke Poland wide open. He worked over here as a heating engineer. On and off. When he wasn't selling stolen scrap metal. Then it was knock-off cars. High-end marques. Stolen to order and never seen in the area again. He'd been in factory maintenance in Poznan. I think he's back there now."

"Plenty of them around, in spite of what you might think." It is Coppinger, breaking off from the sports pages. "Mercs, Jags, Bentleys. Plenty of old money in this part of the country, Sergeant. An aristocracy of many centuries. And not to mention the new money: Londoners mainly, City boys and girls, looking to spend their well-earned bonuses on some trophy manor house with a few acres from the county's extensive property portfolio."

Tufts offers a slight nod and a knowing smile.

"And not just them," the DI goes on. "Have you seen how much bacon a top civil servant is bringing home these days, for Christ's sake?"

Assuming the question is rhetorical, Tufts clears his throat and turns back to Don:

"Is Kermit's mother still around?"

"She was. She brought him up alone. But when I say she brought him up, I'm being generous. She left the county a year or two ago. Kermit doesn't know where she is right now. At least that's what he tells me."

Coppinger looks up from his newspaper again:

"DS Percey, can you get us all some coffee? And a bit of cake from somewhere?"

"Sir."

He knows his boss is showing off but he will ride the wave. Briefly, back to Tufts:

"Kermit has been useful to us in the past. Especially when his back is against the wall."

"He's unreliable," says Coppinger, as if to close down the discussion.

"Well, he can be," says Don, quietly exasperated.

"He's a flaky bastard," insists his boss.

"He doesn't trust anybody. He's learnt not to. Especially the police, most of the time. So far."

"But you're working on it?" asks Tufts

"Among other things..."

"Donny!" shouts Coppinger. "Let him read the fucking file himself. He's from London. He's a clever boy. I'm dying of thirst here! No milk. Two sugars. On your way."

COUNTY HOSPITAL

It's been several days since I wrote. The last section took a lot out of me and I've had bad headaches. They tell me I've been sleeping from mid-afternoons through till the next morning.

I woke up in a heavy sweat, with a nurse (Juliet, I think) holding my hand. It was that dream again: this time I surfaced in the same estuary but it was dark and deserted and the deep water splashing around me was as black as pitch. I felt vulnerable and terribly alone. I must have panicked and started shouting for help.

I know I've been told that I'm writing all this for my own peace of mind, for a voyage of discovery (if that doesn't sound too dramatic), but I also know that this will be read by detectives as they look for a motive - and a suspect - for the attack. My jaw is no longer wired in the same way but it is still painful to speak. I can only manage a few words and I think what I do say is hard to understand. The doctors have given the police very little time with me so far. My mind is still a clutter, but I do get spurts of activity - really intense memories and impressions - and for the moment these words remain my best way of self-expression.

I've just eaten scrambled eggs. It's a delight to be back on solid food (almost) after the drips and tubes. I want to put down in writing here and now my thanks to these nurses. And especially to this pretty one who's just brought me back the laptop. I'll probably get into trouble for saying that.

I was a good detective. I know I was. I always had a sharp eye for detail, and a curiosity that usually went far further than my ability to understand. That's how it was as a kid at school. I loved to read, adventures mainly, but apart from English, everything else was a struggle. In most things I only ever seemed to manage to get halfway. I was advised to give the Sixth Form a swerve and I joined the force as a cadet. The physical stuff was fun, and being a regular bobby had its moments, but I was always more interested in the *why* and the *how* than in the *what*. I applied for CID work quite early on; I was passed over in the first wave but accepted in the next.

Carole said that I was ambitious *only up to a point,* Lord Copper. A funny expression of hers, that. I thought I understood the copper, but not the lord. She told me it was a little phrase from a book by Evelyn Waugh. Whoever *she* was. It's never been my nature to be flamboyant, out there in the limelight. As the job would dictate, I've been on TV (the local news) a few times: requests for information from the general public, statements outside the county court, that sort of thing, but I suppose it's just not me to be loud and self-promoting. I loved to get stuck into a case, do the leg-work, the finger-work, do the background, interviews, statements, scoring clues, exposing motives, solving the puzzle, sensing all the shades of light and dark in a case. I was attuned to all that stuff and was a valuable member of the team. Coppinger's team as it was in the latter years. And happier to be buried in paperwork than out glad-handing. *Social but not sociable.* Carole again, and she was right. I didn't have the urge and never learned the knack of climbing greasy poles. And so it was second fiddle. No hard feelings. I was never likely to be first violin. But I did make DS. Eventually.

My other weakness as a copper, hidden for as long as I could physically hide it, was the grind of coping with mundane violence and its demoralising effects. I was not averse to the physicality of police work. In my early years I could take any rough stuff in my stride and usually emerged with a few bruises and a wide grin. But eventually all that pales and dealing with injuries to myself - and to anyone else - began to cause more and more discomfort. It was low-level stuff in the main: the results of minor assaults, a wife or girlfriend beaten up, animals mistreated. And sometimes the sickening scenes on the next level: drug overdoses and wailing babies, the abused child, the rape victim, the horror of an arson attack. And then the stabbings. And suicide attempts. And murder, of course. I never properly immunised myself from confronting a corpse, neither intact nor mutilated, and I did see a few in my thirty-odd years. Some people manage to block out the human *being* and see only the human *shape*. I never could. I saw only the person and would grieve for their soul.

I still enjoyed the cerebral aspect of detective work, but less and less the aggro, the suffering, the relentless sights and smells of the open wounds of depravity.

It has been a trial working with Edmund Coppinger. And I don't care if he gets to read this; I'm certain he will. A productive, energetic copper, granted, but quite a different beast to me. Which is probably why we were kept together for so long. Two sides of a coin.

In spite of myself I let the age thing get under my skin. Coppinger is two years younger than me, but after his promotion to DI he became my immediate superior. Any mutual respect we had was strained by my resentment, I admit, and by his sarcasm. I used to come home raging more against him than against the villains we were after. But he has a lovely wife and family, and I was genuinely touched when he asked me to be godfather to his eldest son Michael. And as a team we did click: brains meeting brawn is far too simplistic but I believe that without a subtle shift, a change in angle suggested to him, Coppinger would have instinctively worked in straight lines. In return, I concede, he had the clarity to untangle me from many knots of my own making. Of course we disagreed on many things: from musical tastes to the value of cricket, from the use of the apostrophe to the treatment of suspects.

Tommy Krevitz divided us too. Better known as Kermit, here was a boy who needed a helping hand, not a series of slaps. He was a boy-criminal lost in an adult world, making the wrong choices and mixing with the wrong people. Without any real self-confidence he resorted instead to bravado. After early ejection from full-time education and lacking in social skills, he had found no job and he drifted. His parents were a waste of space too: father long absent and mother utterly self-absorbed. Having been instrumental in Kermit's presence at the Young Offenders' Institute, I took an interest in him. I knew he'd have a hard time inside and, sure enough, a botched suicide attempt was reported after less than a month. Nevertheless he survived the ordeal and bounced back on to our radar almost as soon as he was released. I had flagged him up to the youth employment advisory services and tried to persuade Coppinger that he would reform. The DI laughed and told me I was a lousy judge of character and on this one he was right. It wasn't long before Kermit was suspected of being part of a gang that had been breaking into doctors' surgeries in the villages up the valley.

I remember spotting Kermit one morning, quite early, in town with a group of youths. I was crossing the market square, off duty, on my way to the bank, I think. It was a cold morning, winter-time. He was sitting on a moped, surrounded by three or four others, at the corner by the Co-op. All were smoking except for Kermit, who was asthmatic. They wore hoodies and skinny jeans or tracksuit bottoms. One of them, a lad I recognised as Ryan Bayley, was kicking at the moped's back tyre in a daft, playful way, trying to unbalance the rider. He wouldn't have recognised me;

he'd have still been at primary school when I arrested his father. Harry Bayley had been involved in a racket stealing tractors and the like for the second-hand market in somewhere like Croatia or Serbia, I think. He spent years inside but is out now, I'm certain; the word was he'd got divorced and moved to Southampton. Harry Bayley, big ugly sod; we called him Arabella at the station.

Ryan's older sister, I've forgotten her name, now that truly was a sad case. Bright girl, it was her evidence that did for Harry once the prosecution had dismantled her statement. It was a serious charge, attempted GBH, something to do with his in-laws, and she was providing a false alibi for her shit of a dad. Fifteen years old at the time and forced to lie in court. Emotional blackmail. Beverley; that was her name. Bev. It didn't take long for a clever barrister to strip away the lies and Arabella got his ticket to prison. I remember her sobbing her heart out once the dam broke. Mascara smudged down her cheeks like coal dust. She had a full-on breakdown not long after, messed up all of her GCSEs, left school years too soon, was treated on and off for depression, drifted into petty crime and within less than a year had disappeared from the area. The mother blamed the courts for destroying her daughter's spirit; perhaps she should have looked a bit closer to home for somewhere to lay the responsibility. Anyway, that was Bev's story. I hope she's safe, wherever she is now.

I digress. Without really thinking, I was drawn to cross the square towards the group. They were laughing together, mucking about. One lad I didn't recognise saw me before the others and decided to slink away into the alley behind the shops as if I were carrying a disease. I asked Kermit how he was and if he'd seen his mother lately: throwaway questions. The others turned away, looking at the pavement, looking at their cigarettes. Ryan said something under his breath which made the others laugh. Kermit struggled to make eye contact with me, but he did reply in his low, embarrassed mumble, scratching the patchy tufts of blond bristles on his chin. He had had a letter from his mum, as it happened, he said, the first for ages, out of the blue. His dad was back in the country, visiting from Poland, and had asked her to contact their son for him. I asked him if he wanted to see his father. *Dunno,* he said. *Depends. Depends what he wants.*

Then a funny thing happened. I turned to leave him to his mates, reminding him, in a clumsy avuncular way, to keep out of trouble or he'd be a hunted man. But rather than reacting to the humour in my voice, I saw him go rigid, eyelids flickering in a sudden panic as he stared past me. I followed his sight line and spotted a white van on the far side of the square, pausing in the queue of traffic and partially hidden by other cars. I read what Kermit, to his horror, had deciphered - the black lettering high on the van's side: DEATH TRAPZ - PROFESSIONAL KILLERS. Within seconds the traffic edged forwards to reveal the full white boxy shape and the writing below: OF RODENTS AND ALL PESTS. I smiled and looked back in mock relief at Kermit. He still looked blank, hesitating. "They're not coming for *you*, Tommy," I said, and he eventually smiled back, his thin, uncertain smile.

Now I am remembering Paul Tufts. Coppinger and I had many additions to the team over the years, but at a time when we seemed to have been reduced to a fractious double-act, DS Tufts arrived on secondment from Scotland Yard. Clearly a high achiever, he'd been fast-tracked to DS in his mid-twenties and was one to watch. He spent some time at county HQ too, and with the coastal division, but contributed significantly in our department and tried hard to work alongside us without rocking our boat. He had a knack of quickly distilling a problem to its essence and was a clear thinker. He knew his way around a computer system and made me look prehistoric, in spite of all the ICT courses I'd been sent on. I liked him. I liked his modesty. He was something of a closed book but he told me bits and pieces: for example he had a fiancée in Wimbledon. In his spare time he joined a gym, swam fifty lengths of the pool three times a week and practised fencing with a professional coach. He is the only person I have ever met who knows exactly what to do with an épée.

Whereas Coppinger had a head like a potato, Tuft's face was as fresh and as round as a grapefruit. His habit was to wear a suit everyday; one of two he appeared to own, each a different shade of khaki-brown. And everyday a tie of solid colour; no patterns. With his wide, inquisitive pale blue eyes and short, spiky, straw-coloured hair, he reminded me of Tintin. Coppinger preferred to call him, behind his back of course, the Boy Scout.

FOUR

The scene plays in the same minibus. The lanes are covered with fallen leaves, damp and gluey in the gutters. It feels like a morning in October and the children are missing, already dropped off at school. Don is on his way back, eschewing the muddy back lanes for the direct route to town.

"Polo was very subdued this morning," he is saying to Rita, his only passenger, who has removed her fluorescent outer layer and is now sitting by him in the front seats sucking a mint.

"Yes, I've seen him like that before. He doesn't want to talk. Under a cloud. Best to ignore him. He'll go to the back of the bus and stare out of the window. He had his PlayStation today, you probably noticed."

"I could hear it."

"I told him to turn the sound down but he wasn't havin' any. He turns it down a bit and then a minute later it's up again. Horrible noise - crashin' and screechin'. God knows what the lad's watchin'. It does upset the little ones."

"He could do with some earphones. Keep the noise to himself."

Rita spots someone she knows waiting at a bus stop and waves exaggeratedly, but they are already past him and he was daydreaming.

"Jocky's friend. I don't think he saw me."

Don has no idea who Jocky is, never mind his friend.

"He'll probably be a bit happier this afternoon," she resumes.

"Who's that?"

"Polo."

Don slows the bus down as they approach a junction.

"What was his mum saying to you?" he asks after a moment. "Have they had a row?"

"No, not as far as I know. Well, not her and Polo. His dad is back, mind you. Malcolm. That was his car, the white one, parked at the end of their lane."

Don remembers seeing the car, fairly new, sunroof; he'd had to swing further out into the hedge to avoid it.

"I thought you said he'd left her and gone to live in London."

"Well, he did, but he comes back now and again. Usually when the work dries up or his latest girlfriend kicks him out."

"So how long is he staying this time?"

"I don't know, but not for long, probably. Not if Geena's got anythin' to do with it. He hit her last night."

"Did he? Did she tell you that?"

"Yeah, she showed me a black eye. All swollen up. I don't suppose you saw that."

"No. I did notice she was wearing sunglasses. And had she changed her hair colour or was that my imagination?"

Don has clunked down a couple of gears to attack a sharp rise on a bend. Rita doesn't answer. She probably hasn't heard him over the engine noise.

"Yes, the glasses," he continues, a little more loudly. "I did think it was a bit odd. You know, it's quite a bright morning, but she looked like she'd been wearing them indoors."

"She was hidin' her black eye from the kids, I expect. But Polo must have known. He's not daft. He knows what Malcolm's like."

"How is he with his father?"

"I don't really know. When he's around he talks about him a lot, what they get up to together, you know. But then he'll go back off to London or wherever and Polo just seems to forget about him. You'll probably see him this afternoon. Geena's in work today, she was tellin' me, so he'll probably meet him off the bus instead."

"Oh, right. Is he Angelo's dad as well?"

"Angelo's? No. I don't know who *his* dad is. You do see different men around here from time to time."

"Like the bloke with the camper van and the dogs?"

"Oh, God, yes!" laughs Rita. "I don't think he'll be back."

"Really?"

"I think Geena soon got fed up feedin' his dogs. And he was a funny lookin' fella anyway, wasn't he?"

"You mean his wig?"

"Well, his daft wig and his daft furry boots. He wore them indoors, she said. No, I can't keep track. You never know who's comin' or goin'. But she's never said about Angelo's father. Well, not to me. Malcolm's Polo and Amber's dad. Just the last two."

"Are they married, him and Geena?"

"No, no. They're not wed. I think it's a bit too late for all that! She'll not marry again. At least that's what she told me. But she does change her mind, does Geena."

And as the picture fades, Rita's voice trails away with it: "Almost as often as she changes her hair dye."

Juliet wheeled me out on to a patio this morning and I sat in the sunshine for a while. Or was it this afternoon? I don't know. My sleep patterns are messed up and my sense of time is very wobbly. I have been remembering my dreams less and less in recent days, but a new one on the escalator keeps recurring: the same short scenario, on a silent rolling staircase in an empty shopping mall somewhere exotic. There are potted palms and orchids everywhere and the scent of jasmine and ginger and, weirdly, diesel fumes from an engine that invisibly drives the stairs forever forwards. I am in India, probably, or Singapore. For some reason I am convinced, when I am in the dream, that it's Singapore. I have never been to Singapore. And the escalator is sometimes up, but mostly down. Up or down, I can never seem to get off it.

I haven't had the dream in the lake for at least a week. The last time I had it I surfaced in what appeared to be a fish-pond: it was the fish-pond in my son Gabriel's garden, and there I was, seeing myself playing cricket on the small garden lawn with Gabe, who was a little boy. And the figures kept shifting, so that now Gabe was the adult tossing a ball towards his own son, Oliver, who swished wildly with the toy bat, squealing and missing the ball every time. And then suddenly it wasn't Oliver at all, it was Polo Dale, the boy on the bus, playing cricket in my son's garden, swishing and missing every time, swishing and missing and getting more and more frustrated and angry and sweary and red in the face, until I finally woke up with a throat that was as dry as dust.

Juliet has told me that she is from Ghana, a country I could probably have a good stab at pointing to on a map. Find Nigeria on the Atlantic corner of the continent and work west a bit. I remember looking at the maps of the world in my father's stamp album when I was a young boy. His particular interest was stamps of the British Empire and most of his collection was from that time in the post-war years when much of Africa was still shaded in imperial pink and Ghana was still called the Gold Coast. I thought it sounded like a brilliant place to live, with bits of precious metal lying on every beach. Much better than the Ivory Coast or the Grain Coast. Poor Juliet tried to teach me a little about her country but I am not a great listener at the moment. When she comes to me first thing in the morning to check my levels and bring pain relief I have started calling her my Ghanaian Angel; I'm not sure where that came from but it's a joke she seems to like. And she swears she hasn't heard it before.

Anyway, while I was out on the patio, breathing in the mild summer air, I do remember that John Pattermore came to see me. He didn't stay long, but I did acknowledge him with nods and waves. It was kind of him to visit, and it reminded me of the minibus job and the rides along the country lanes with Rita.

The children we took to school were delightful. They had their little tantrums and their moods, but who couldn't forgive them for an odd fractious five minutes? Some days we had songs or nursery rhymes, some days *I Spy* which was riotously absurd with so few of them knowing their letters. There were daft jokes and silly stories that tailed off into nonsense. We heard details of parents' lives we really shouldn't have been told. And we heard snippets of parents' conversation that had been cut and pasted into their own ingenuous lexicon, loaded, knowing phrases in the mouths of babes: *What-ever, What's all that about? Deal with it!* for example, and *I can't talk right now* (perfect for a child undergoing speech therapy, I thought). Often in the afternoon one or two would fall asleep. It was a lovely, easy job. No anxiety. No stress unless we got stuck behind a slow tractor on a narrow lane. After a lifetime trying to make some sense of spite, vindictiveness and criminality, of trying to restore a sense of justice to victims of an endless flow of nastiness, it felt like I'd scrambled out of a dark, swampy jungle and emerged on to the slopes of bright, sunlit uplands.

It took me no time to realise that the most interesting of the children was Polo Dale. He was the oldest and had the most to say. He could be sulky, he could be rude and he could be funny. His mood could change like the wind. One day he stepped on to the bus hating his mother because she had sent him to bed early the previous evening. So we had nasty, vicious curses. Not a word of hello to Rita. When we arrived home in the afternoon, he jumped off the bus and gave his mum a big hug. They ran into the house together, laughing, Polo squealing as he tried to escape her tickles. One day he swore at Rita and was made to apologise. I know he didn't mean it. He was angry about something else, probably an argument with his older brother, and he exploded on the bus over something and nothing. He was genuinely ashamed at upsetting Rita, I think, because it was obvious to me that he adored her.

One afternoon that autumn I met his father, Malcolm. He was a large man with fleshy arms and brown tufty hair like Polo's. He was wearing a black tee-shirt with a Batman logo and a pair of paint-stained beach-shorts. He was sitting in the sun in a deck-chair on the patch of grass outside the front door, smoking a roll-up. He did not get up as I parked the minibus, waiting until Polo had got off. I had the impression that he didn't want to have to speak to Rita. He couldn't avoid meeting my eyes, however, and we exchanged the briefest of pleasantries in neutral tones. Polo threw his bag on to the deck-chair, said he was thirsty, and walked into the house. With the front door open, the smells from inside offered stale tinned soup with a hint of cat litter.

Rita was a mine of information about many things although she rarely spoke to me about her husband. She had lived in town all of her sixty years and she knew just enough about everybody that mattered. She knew all that was wrong with the county's school transport system and had most of the solutions to fix it. If only the suits in County Hall had bothered to ask her. She was also a good listener and I found it easy to talk to her about myself, about my work in the police, about my family, even about losing Carole. She was most useful to me in feeding my natural curiosity in the children and their families. Notably in the Dale family.

Geena Dale was pale and slim, had a tired but girlish face, and was forty years old. Polo told us that himself on her birthday. And that she was going to tell people she was thirty-nine for a good few years yet. Her parents had been travellers and she had spent much of her childhood among caravans and campfires, dialect, disobedience and dogs. She had her first child, Kenny, when she was sixteen, and had married the father shortly afterwards. They divorced a couple of years later and Geena never spoke of him. Rita thought he had left the area years ago. Kenny was a source of some pride, however. He joined the army straight from school and had spent two lengthy stints in Afghanistan. When back in England he did visit his mother occasionally, and the last time he brought back a war game for Polo for his PlayStation. I later discovered that although his service in the army was to be admired, he had in the past developed a reputation as being something of a bully.

Geena's second son was Angelo. He was a feckless youth who left school as soon as he could about two years ago. Still unemployed and trained for nothing, he had nevertheless managed to get his girlfriend pregnant and had thus rendered Geena a grandmother, for which he received no thanks. Apparently her irritation melted away the moment she first held the newborn, stared into its tiny pink scrunched-up face and smelled the sweet essence of a baby girl, Lily, her first granddaughter. Angelo is far from the model father, spending only a little time with mother and daughter, a little more scrounging off his mother and living under her roof, and even more on the streets of the town both late at night and at the crack of dawn. Angelo's own father was not known to Rita, but as she said, the field was quite an open one.

Next came Malcolm, part-time painter and decorator, part-time Londoner, father of Polo and six year-old Amber. Amber Dale was thriving at school and loved to read. Geena had complained to Rita that she *could never get her to put her bloody books down and come for her tea!* The girl suffers from asthma, and Polo announced to us one day that she now had a new pink inhaler. I wondered if it had occurred to the mother that so many smokers puffing away in the house was not helpful; she smoked and so did Angelo, Polo said, not to mention the trail of visitors passing through. Including Malcolm, now back in my mind's eye, sitting down in his deck-chair again, waving goodbye to us with one hand like a carefree country squire, and shading his eyes from the sun with the other. Mr Punch to Geena's Judy?

I remember imagining Polo sitting in the house waiting for his mum to come home from work. He would be watching television with a can of Coke. He never seemed to have any homework to do. And eventually she would come home, in her cheap summer dress and cardigan, sunglasses over dark tired eyes, behind the wheel of a pale blue people-carrier past middle-age (03-reg) with its near-side wing-mirror missing. Of all the occupants of the five homes that made up The Pavilions, Geena was the only one who had a job, she told Rita with some pride: not a full-time job, but something at the cheese factory, just part-time so as not to affect her state benefits - three afternoons a week, packing slabs of cheddar. It was just enough to get her out of the house, enough to keep the family in new shoes and maybe have a week in a holiday camp in the summer.

Riding home in a seat directly behind me one afternoon, Polo told me about a holiday he remembered - not last year, he was certain - on a campsite on the Isle of Wight. He thought it was called the Island White. Rita said that Geena had taken them out of school before the end of term so she could catch the cheaper season rates for a chalet. Polo had enjoyed it even though the site was half-empty. His mum had paid a man to take them sea-fishing. They had eaten a lot of chips. Angelo hadn't wanted to come and had moaned all week. Polo knew quite a good deal about fishing, fresh water mainly; he called it *angling* and said that he was saving up for a proper rod and line. He said he'd nobody to go with but it didn't matter because you could have just as much fun on your own. He told me that all the friends he used to have in the village were snobs. I said I'd take him fishing - *sorry, angling* - to the lake near my house one day if his mum would let him come. I don't know why I said that as I never believed it would happen and wasn't even sure that I wanted it to. Or even if I was allowed to, come to think of it. Child protection, etc.

One day on the way home from school I was listening to him talking to Rita. The other children were dozing. He had spotted a V-formation of geese flying over the valley and described it as *an arrowhead*. Another day he remarked quite suddenly that the late angled sunlight on a grassy field in the distance made it look like *velvet*. And one freezing cold morning I had to smile when, seeing the hedges in the lane ahead of us covered in thick hoar frost, he claimed that all the branches and leaves looked like they'd been *dusted with sugar in the night-time*.

In the early weeks Polo still used to torment us with the noise from his PlayStation. I found an old pair of earphones at home, probably Gabe's from years ago, and handed them to him one day. The tinny noise was immediately reduced and everybody was happy. Later that afternoon as I was parking outside his house, he gave them back to me, thinking I had simply let him borrow them for the day. When I insisted that he could keep them, his eyes sprang wide open and his smile was even broader. Rita prompted him to thank me. Then he jumped down from the bus and ran across the grass, kicking away an empty beer can, to show Amber his new prize.

FIVE

The scene plays in an airless operations room in a familiar police station. DS Paul Tufts is sitting at a computer screen, quietly tapping at a keyboard, watching intently as a new matrix of numbers and shapes appears before his ice-blue eyes. Standing at his shoulder, sharing the view and looking faintly bemused is Don. He scratches his head and makes light of his confusion:

"I'm entirely in your hands on this one, Paul," he says. "If you can make head or tail of that lot then you're a better man than me!"

Tufts types a combination of keys but makes no answer beyond a soft gasp of frustration as the screen produces a new page of coded data. Don stretches his arms like he's a crucifix, lets out a long sigh and casts his gaze around the rest of the room.

"Hey, Don! Come over here! Look at this!"

It is the voice of a junior techie sitting at a monitor on the far side of the room by the blinded windows, someone who should call him sergeant or even sir, some cheeky computer wizard with a stained open-neck shirt and cheap aftershave who thinks that he can play by his own rules.

"Ain't this someone you know?"

Don walks over to see what the fuss is about. The young

51

officer swivels his seat around to greet him, flicking a gobbet of chewing gum out of his mouth and into a bin at his feet.

"Not sure how well you know her, Don," he laughs, tilting the screen. "Or how well you'd like to know her, if you get me…"

Don finds himself staring at a middle-aged woman talking to a webcam in what appears to be her bedroom. The sound is muted but the gist of her suggestions is clear. She moves away from the camera with the flash of a smile and perches on the end of a double bed. She is wearing only a flimsy black bra, a miniskirt, a leather wristband and a fake tan.

"She's a neighbour of yours, ain't she, Don?"

"Call me *sir* if it's not too much bother."

"Sorry, sir. Ain't she, though?"

"As a matter of fact, she is."

Don recognises Gaynor Otterbridge and is lost for words. Mrs Otterbridge from next door. From number eight. Mrs Otterbridge who works at the garage shop selling petrol and newspapers. What the hell?

"That's Gaynor Otterbridge," he says at last.

"Yes, we know who it is, sir. She goes by the name of Isabella online. Apparently. We know where she lives, what she's up to."

The young man cannot stifle a snigger and Don's own expression is thawing into a smile of disbelief. The woman on the screen, still talking silently to the webcam, is loosening her bra, fondling her breasts beneath the lace, tossing her head back in mock delight, shaking her thick auburn hair in a flourish. Her eyes, trained on the watchers', perform but they are strangely dead, thinks Don: she knows this tawdry pantomime is beneath her, he is thinking, and more than a deadness, it's a sadness in her eyes he thinks he can read.

"There ain't nothing illegal here, sir, but vice came across her while they were doing a net trawl. Somebody recognised her as a local woman. Pinged it over to us for a laugh."

The woman is removing her bra, giggling to the lens, brandishing her fleshy bosom to the watching world. She pirouettes and bends over to reveal her wiggling backside, as bare as the day she was born but for a tiny black thong. Then suddenly she is back in close-up with a pink blouse on, talking to the camera as she brushes her hair; the video is on a loop.

"One of them spotted her as a neighbour of yours, Don. Sir. Thought you'd be interested. Well, curious at least."

"It's a side to her I haven't seen before, that's for sure. We usually talk about the bin collection or the weather or just lately her husband's new shed."

"I wonder if her hubby knows what she gets up to."

"Quite."

And suddenly a new voice:

"Donny, where's Tufts disappeared to, for Christ's sake?"

It is Coppinger, shouting to him from the open doorway.

"I didn't have you down as the kind of perv who watches that kind of thing, Sergeant!"

And just for a moment Don is embarrassed, not by the moving images of the sultry Gaynor Otterbridge but by the fact that he hasn't even noticed that DS Tufts had left the room.

*

The scene plays in the same police station on another day. DI Edmund Coppinger's excitable voice once more fills the room: his own office where he sits like an emperor beneath a signed white England rugby shirt in a large glass frame; his hair longer now, bordering scruffy.

"DS Percey!" he barks through the open door. "Get your arse in here and look at these lovelies!"

And now Don appears at the doorway. This room is still stalked by the ghost of stale tobacco, a reminder of the days when cigarettes were lit up inside and smoke hung in the air like a constant veil.

"What's on your mind, sir?"

Coppinger is leaning back in his padded swivel chair, his face bearing the expression of a man whose lottery numbers have just come up.

"These have just come through via Scout," he declares, pointing at the computer screen on his desk. "The ferrets downstairs have been trawling through Joyner's recycle bin."

Beckoning to Don to join him on his side of the desk, he shifts the angle of the monitor towards him. Don notices first the pair of framed photographs of Coppinger's family: a studio group of four posed self-consciously in smart-casuals and next to it a head-and-shoulders of his smiling wife.

"Look what some clever scavenger has unscrambled. A link between Somers and Kermit. So far we've been guessing, and Kermit's a slippery bastard, but here he is, a walking talking Class A-dealing superstar in his very own glitzy online show!"

Don reads the neat print of first one short e-mail, then, pasted directly below it on the screen, a second:

11 December

TO: *Somers, Lawrence*

FROM: *Jason Joyner jjoynerjj@beemail.com*

SUBJECT: *Polish*

Hi, Laurie

Have you heard from the Pole since last week? What a bloody cheek asking if he can supply you with goods! I agree he needs to be reminded of the reality of the marketplace. Happy to oblige.

See you at the weekend.

I believe Susan has invited Immie and me over for lunch on Saturday.

Looking forward to it.

Jay

5 January

TO: *Jason Joyner jjoynerjj@beemail.com*

FROM: *Somers, Lawrence*

SUBJECT: *RE. Polish*

Our Polish friend is becoming a fucking pest. He has ignored your warnings and is still wanting to negotiate from what he says is a position of strength. He's bluffing, of course. I guess his supplier has cut him off and he wants to create a good impression on me. From what I hear he is still selling locally and is treading on toes. It's time for a more persuasive approach. But be careful who you involve.

L.

"These are a month apart," says Don. "Is there anything else in between, sir?"

"Not that I know," replies Coppinger, pulling himself up from his slouch. "Nothing incriminating in any case. Not unless Tufts is keeping them to himself. If you read his note, there, on this next page, he reckons these are the only two they've found re Polish."

"It could be any Pole, sir."

"Yeah, it could be any Pole. It could be the Pope, but he's dead. It could be Lech Walesa himself, of course. But he doesn't live here and I don't believe he's acquainted with Laughing Boy. It's Kermit, for fuck's sake! I know we've had him in before, scared him shitless, but he's always had a story. Always managed to jump back into his pond."

Don is edging away from the desk, away from the monitor, instinctively putting distance between himself and the force of Coppinger's inevitability.

"He has done a stretch at the YOI," he offers.

"Yeah, well. We've all moved along since those days, Don."

"He managed to jump back into his pond, as you put it, because although he appears fragile, he's stronger than he looks. And, by the way, we had no evidence to convict him."

"Look, Don, I know the kid is one you have a soft spot for, but face facts. Read these e-mails again if the penny hasn't dropped."

Don, for whom reading them once is enough, looks his boss directly in the eyes.

"I agree, this is incriminating stuff."

"Well, exactly."

"There's no mention of Kermit, though, not by name, and no mention of drugs, Class A or otherwise, or stolen goods at all…"

"He's not trying to sell Somers fucking washing machines!"

"That would be unlikely, granted. But you see my point."

"No I don't see your point," retorts Coppinger. He is losing patience and there is more purpose in his voice. "But what I do want to see is Kermit's arse under the grill. We can pick him up today. He sleeps at home most afternoons, doesn't he?"

"That has been his habit in the last few months, sir."

"Well, then. Ring Tufts and get him round as soon as."

"DS Tufts is in London today, sir, remember. Two days, isn't it, till the end of the week…?

"Right, never mind him." Coppinger is already on his feet, fastening the buttons of his jacket. "I'll take two of the uniform lads with me."

"I'll come with you, sir," suggests Don. "We'll need to play it carefully."

Affronted, Coppinger shoots him a steely glance.

"What the hell you men? I *can* do 'carefully', sergeant."

"Yes, sir. Sorry." Don is standing in the doorway, an obstacle to his boss without meaning to be but an obstacle nonetheless. "But you know how Kermit is. Kid gloves recommended. Sledgehammer and we'll break him up before we get the chance to break him open."

"Thanks for the advice, Don, but if we can nail Somers with this then I don't fucking care if we have one broken stooge on our hands. Deal with it. He'll mend."

I am never sure if they are flashbacks or dreams. I can't even remember if I am ever conscious when they come clunking into my mind. I have lost track of the drugs they've been pumping into my system. But they stay with me, these vivid, shifting scenes, some amusing, others more troubling.

I think it must have been the shock of seeing my neighbour Mrs Otterbridge indulging in a soft-porn striptease that has made it an image that reoccurs: especially being in high-definition megapixels on a police computer screen. It was about the time that Tufts and his techies were trying to break open Jason Joyner's encrypted e-mail account.

Although she is several years past her prime as an object of desire, it has to be said that Gaynor is still what people sometimes describe as a *handsome woman*. I have absolutely no idea if she is still using her bedroom as a film set. At the time, however, I suppose she must have known what she was doing: she had the tech, the lighting, the lingerie and she must have been charging the punters plenty to watch her performance to make the whole thing worth her while. Enough to pay for her weekly shop, perhaps. A proper little cottage industry. Or maybe she did it, does it, just for fun, with or without the profit motive. Looking back, it's a shame Carole knew nothing of her initiative; she always admired creative friends who had the gumption to self-publish. Mostly writers, though, naturally. I don't think she ever knew anybody in the world of show business. It was down to me, of course, that she never knew. Did I just wrap it all up as *work* and keep it to myself, or were we going through one of those spells at the time when each one of the rare words we exchanged seemed barbed? Gaynor was, is, only a neighbour, after all.

In any event it made our next encounter over the garden hedge a little strained. She was wearing a lot less make-up and the lines of age had free rein on her face. Her hands were grubby and her hair looked colourless and tired. I hadn't really paid any attention to her hair before; it struck me then that the persona of Isabella came with a lustrous wig. She wore a shapeless old jumper and a pair of jeans tucked into her wellingtons. She had been digging up a line of shrubs and had worked up quite a sweat. We both said *hi* in our usual non-committal way and nothing more for a few seconds. She was in the middle of explaining how she was making room for her husband's shed to be extended when she suddenly stopped talking and looked at me quizzically. Was I wearing a creepily frozen expression? Had I been staring at her chest? *I think I've got a bug in my eye*, she said. *Can you see anything, Don?* I remember offering to dab it out with the corner of a tissue I found in my pocket, delicately holding her cheek with my free hand, the warm, damp cheek of secret Isabella, the face so discreetly familiar to her multitude of private viewers, even though they would mostly be ogling the other bits of her. The last time I saw her was at the supermarket, pushing a trolley down the aisle. I was half expecting to find her buying make-up or underwear or scented candles and, in the end, was both relieved and yet disappointed that I caught her in the act of selecting a cauliflower.

I'd never had much time for her husband, a stunted weasel of a man. Alec Otterbridge runs a two-man plumbing business with his wife's son. From a previous marriage, I assume. Forgotten the lad's name. In his late twenties, I would say. Not that I get too snotty about these things (Carole was much worse), but when he had his front lawn paved over and then most of his back garden razed to put up the ugliest of garages-cum-garden sheds for his off-roader, the upheaval impacted on the whole close, not just on us as his nearest neighbours: huge sacks of gravel and sand spilling onto the pavement for weeks, a rusting skip of rubble at the kerbside. I don't think that planning permission crossed his mind; it did cross Carole's, but everybody ended up being very English about it all and let him get on with it through gritted teeth. *The sooner he finishes, the better.*

He races at rallycross, or at least he used to. I think he sold the 4x4 when his business was going through a sticky patch and he bought a second-hand quad-bike instead. I remember him coming over as a favour to repair the stopcock on our water tank in the attic one Christmas Eve: a fifteen-minute job. I gave him a very decent bottle of wine as a thank you; he really had saved our bacon. Then about a week later we received in the post (*in the post!*) an invoice from Otterbridge & Banks Services for £75 parts and labour + VAT. We never had much to say to each other after that, Alec and I.

I must have fallen asleep watching the Test match on TV. The last thing I remember was England making heavy weather of batting on what looked like a decent wicket. Next thing I know, we're fielding again.

Gabe arranged for the television; he pulled a few strings. I think he felt guilty about going on holiday next week and leaving me alone, not that I will be. They're going to Brittany, just for a week; booked it ages ago. Gabe was all for cancelling, what with me in such a state, but everyone says I'm more or less on the mend, ahead of schedule, physiotherapy due to be extended, soon be back in the pink, etc. I insisted they go. They all need a break. Especially Gabe, coming in here with a long face every single day.

Was Detective Sergeant Paul Tufts sent to the county with the deliberate aim of nailing men like Lawrence Somers?

I never knew for sure. Certainly his secondment from the Met wasn't just to offer him respite from unremitting urban knife crime and instead to afford him a gentle introduction to the lower profile detective work involved in solving red diesel theft from farmyard storage tanks. Nevertheless, Kermit was heavy-priced collateral damage for our upping of the ante.

Lawrence Somers, sometimes Laurie but never Larry, was a long-time suspect of ours in the distribution of drugs (a little Class A, a lot more Class B) in not only our patch but our near neighbours' too. A meticulous man, he allegedly hid these operations behind a legitimate electricals business, the fruit of three generations of Somers. As a mid-sized independent rival to the major high-volume retailers, the business had managed to maintain and even extend its niche as a local, trusted "family" concern whose customer service could always knock spots of the faceless giants squatting by the ring roads. There was a branch of the business run by his son-in-law, Jason Joyner, which bought and sold sophisticated electronic equipment: mostly legitimate, but it was rumoured that you could get a spy camera or a bugging device from Joyner if you spoke the right language and could pay cash. Somers himself encouraged their use, allegedly, opening the door to blackmail cases involving his own rivals and enemies. In any event the suspicions were that Laurie's lifestyle was supported by larger funds than even a successful enterprise trading in white goods could be providing. It is one thing to hide money away but quite another to conceal what you're spending it on.

It is a coincidence that Lawrence Somers had made his home in Geena Dale's village, but the rambling collection of farm buildings, renovated to the highest of bespoke specifications, was as far removed from The Pavilions as you could possibly get. Formerly known as Badgers Farm, he renamed it Somers Set - this always struck me as the height of clever smugness. The indoor pool plus sauna was flanked by a three-acre paddock and stables in which were pampered a pair of chestnut thoroughbreds, the property of Mrs Susan Somers, Laurie's wife of thirty-five storm-tossed years. Lately rebranding herself, with a nod of affection to her deceased father, as Mrs Somers-Pippin, she was less likely to be sighted trotting through the village lanes on horseback, however, than bruising the speed limit in her *solar orange* Audi TT on the 303 en route for shopping opportunities in Knightsbridge. DI Coppinger had long considered Mrs Somers to be the Achilles heel of her husband; one day her indulgences would lead to a slip, he reckoned, a lapse in concentration that would allow access to his bank accounts and a degree of bullying in one of our interview rooms. We knew he had offshore accounts, but he'd had all his tax affairs expertly tidied up and filed away; his finances seemed unwieldy but absolutely watertight.

Instead it was a lead investigated by DS Tufts into the philandering of Somers' son-in-law which moved the case apace. Jason Joyner, husband of Somers' only child Imogen, had been promoted upon marriage from branch manager to a company directorship and a role as head of operations in the expansion of the business into the county to our west. Enlarging Joyner's sphere of influence as a sop to his daughter was a rare example of Somers taking his eye off the ball. Before too long Jason began to mix business with pleasure and was caught in the bedroom of a solicitor's wife with his silk boxers literally round his ankles. Confronted by the solicitor and not in the best position to deny guilt, he foolishly started to throw his weight about and both men had already suffered broken noses before the wife called the police. Backing up her husband's version of events, she left Jason with nowhere to go but to court, charged not only with aggravated assault but also possession of more cocaine than could be seriously claimed to be for personal use. Tufts ensured that Joyner's laptop was seized, which lead to the discovery of hundreds of pirated music CDs, DVDs and computer games at his home. More importantly, a pair of deleted e-mails involving Lawrence Somers and a Pole was retrieved.

Joyner was sent down for eighteen months, I remember; no doubt he'll be out by now, but I expect he remains a persona non grata in the Somers family. Who would feel more betrayed: deceived wife or implicated father-in-law? As far as I know, Laurie had to resort to erecting some expensive legal mazes which continue to leave the police staring at dead ends. But by that time, mercifully, I was well out of the picture.

If you have ever tried to break an egg by pressing down on it from the top, you will know how the thin shell is protected by its design. Press on it from the sides, though, and it will burst like a soap bubble. The angle of approach is everything.

I'd already had more than enough of Coppinger and the incident with Kermit was the last straw for me. For some reason we drove to his flat separately. Coppinger took with him a pair of beat officers he found on a break in the canteen. I drove alone but, while taking what I knew was normally a quicker route, was caught up in temporary traffic lights. Then I had to pull over to answer a phone call from Carole: something and nothing, but you never know. Why didn't she just text? Anyway, by the time I'd found a parking space outside the flats, Coppinger must have been up there with Kermit for nearly ten minutes.

I had visited this flat before and could imagine the scene. Kermit would be sweating, buzzing with nerves, adrenalin unfogging a headache he'd have had from being awoken suddenly from daytime sleep. He'd need his medication, but Coppinger wouldn't give him that option.

Kermit had lived most of his life in this fifth-floor apartment with his mother, until she left him a couple of years ago to take up with a man she'd met on holiday who owned a boat-yard. That's another story. It was a small one-bedroom flat in a block of about twenty-five, the only high-rise of this type in the whole town; this a mistake of planning rectified before more were built. As far as I could tell, Kermit still slept on the sofa pull-out. His mother's old bedroom was kept padlocked. There was an airless bathroom and a tiny kitchenette. I had poked my head into both, briefly, for neither was edifying. On the corner of the ceiling there was a patch of damp, faded brown like an old gravy stain. The sink was half-full of unwashed dishes and cider bottles. I remember too a large flat-screen TV and a top-of-the-range DVD player dominating the living space. The floor was of cheaply treated cement, painted brown and stained, covered near the sofa by a small beige fluffy rug. When I had questioned him there about some small-scale garage break-in, he sat staring past me, shaking, fidgeting, tugging at clumps of his thin, spiky hair and for some moments at a time picking up a sheet of old newspaper from a large pile and tearing up into tiny neat strips which fell to the floor like home-made confetti. That's classic behaviour to help distract and settle the nerves, according to a friend of mine who thought he knew something about psychology. And instead of a window, Kermit had the luxury of a pair of glass doors which opened up on to a narrow balcony, which itself gave on to the car park below.

So, I can imagine the scene:

Kermit on the defensive from the outset, gibbering, pushed one way then the other by Coppinger's hammer-head questions. One of the uniforms threatens to break open the locked bedroom door. Do they even have a warrant? *How do you know Lawrence Somers? Did he sell you that fancy TV? Did you ever sell him anything? How's your mother?*

How's your father? Back in Poland screwing his way through every prostitute in Poznan? Has Lawrence Somers ever been in this flat? Smells bad in here, don't it? What's behind that door? Anything you want to tell me? Why did your mother leave you to rot in this shitty hole, Kremitz? Is it because you're such a fucking loser? Some of this, according to one of the uniforms a day later, was spat out by Coppinger verbatim.

I turned from locking my car and looking up to the fifth floor I noticed that Kermit's balcony doors were wide open. I could even see the slight movement of a grey-green curtain inside. I thought I heard a scream, a shrill desperate squeal, but it could have been the air brakes of a lorry in the distance. Or my imagination. I needed to be up there.

I started to run and was three or four yards from the entrance to the building when, from above, I caught a dark blur in the corner of my eye, felt a draught of air, and before I had an instant to react, I was knocked to the ground by the glancing blow of a flailing body which landed with a hideous crack and thump at my feet. It was like being struck by a flying laundry basket. Meanwhile the thin, plasticky rattle of a small object bouncing off the concrete and rolling away into the gutter caught my attention: a cracked blue inhaler. It took me a couple of seconds to sit myself up and realise that Kermit was lying on his back inches from me, groaning weakly. His limbs were distorted, he'd lost a shoe, and his head was twisted at the neck. His eyes were open and the blood flowing through broken teeth on to his jaw and cheeks made his pale skin look more sallow than ever. As I crawled towards him, I swear he was breathing but he couldn't answer his name and moments later his short, desperate breaths weakened and then faded to nothing. A small shallow pool of blood was leaking from an ear, framing his skull like a scarlet halo.

I heard shouts from people above.

The sight of a man, inert and broken, another man in a

series of lost, damaged men I'd known, made me feel faint, sour and nauseous. Kermit's blood was on my trousers and the sleeve of my jacket. It felt as though it was in my hair, my eyes, cold and salty and ferric inside my mouth. I needed to go home, wash it all away and then wash it all away again. I staggered to my feet and took a huge gasp of air, breathing in until my ribs hurt. Any hesitancy I had previously felt vanished in that moment. My mind was made up: I'd had enough of the police. Call me over-sensitive, call me a quitter, but I wanted to jump ship there and then, to swim far away to a tropical island where I could breathe in lungfuls of clean air, feel the warm sun on my face and live on fresh pineapples forever.

SIX

The scene plays in the same minibus. The children are quiet, Rita is texting somebody, the engine growls as the bus decelerates to avoid an outsized tractor rumbling up the lane towards it, churning up the sodden earth of the verge, spitting up pellets of mud from its tyre-tracks. It's a damp, misty morning and the air is cold. The bus's heater is doing its best but the draughts it is straining to offer are barely warm. With a gloved hand Don flicks on the windscreen washers to clear the splashes of brown dirt from his view. A couple of the children are drawing matchstick figures in the condensation on the windows. The bus rolls on, skirting the dark channels of over-running winterbournes, over a narrow river bridge, winding through the lanes with their tall, trimmed hedges and stony passing places. As it lurches by the gatehouse to an unnamed country manor hidden from view by several acres of sloping woodland, a pair of voices fade in to fill the air.

"Your mum was in good spirits this mornin', Polo."

"She's like that sometimes."

"She said your dad would be stayin' for a good while longer."

Polo is looking out of the window distractedly.

"Mm."

Don likes listening to the boy's conversations with Rita. The woman puts her phone back into her bag. It's the sloppy canvas bag that contains her roll of tissues, her wet-wipes, her bottle of disinfectant, her clutch of paper sick-bags, her rudimentary first aid kit, her pair of pale blue latex gloves. It holds her note-pad and stubby pencil, her bright orange waterproof jacket rolled into a sausage, her thin folder of confidential documentation, her tatty book of crossword puzzles for when our conversation lulls, her half-filled bottle of mineral water and her little packet of barley sugars.

"That'll be nice," she goes on, addressing the boy but facing forwards. "Havin' your dad around again for a bit, I reckon."

"Mm."

"Maybe he'll stay for Christmas. That'd be nice, wouldn't it, Polo, havin' Christmas with all your family together?"

Polo has already had enough of this conversation. Rita isn't pressing. She knows what he's like. Eventually he says:

"He said he'd buy me a bike."

"Did he?"

"A red BMX, like the one I got nicked, only new."

"Didn't your bike ever turn up then?"

"No."

"That was weeks ago, wasn't it?"

"Yeah."

"Just taken from right outside your house…"

"It's gone. I don't really care now."

"Don't think you'll get it back?"

"Dad says he'll get me a new one."

"You'll have to be a good boy, Polo. Help your mum, no playin' up…"

Then, quite out of the blue, a third voice, the chirrup of a little girl:

"I've got a bike."

It's Emily, from under layers of knitwear.

"Have you, Emily?" says Rita, turning in her seat to see her better.

"Yes. I've got."

"And what colour is your bike then?"

"I've got a bike, Polo," she adds, as if for emphasis.

"Is it a red one, Emily?" asks Rita.

The child screws up her nose in thought before giving up:

"Forgot."

She rubs her chin, just like she has seen her daddy do, trying hard to remember. Suddenly, from the back of the bus:

"Pheasant!"

Reece is bouncing on his seat, threatening to come out of his belt, pointing towards a vague target in the fields outside.

"Reece has seen a pheasant, has he?" wonders Rita aloud. "Where is it, Reece, my love? I can't see one. Mind you, my window is all steamed up."

"There!" shouts the boy. "Pleasant! In the field!"

"Oh, yes, there it is. Can you see the pheasant, Cameron? Reece has got very good eyesight, hasn't he?"

Don casts a glance in his rear-view mirror. Reece is still bouncing up and down. Cameron is straining to see through the mist. Emily is buried under a woolly hat. Polo turns in his seat to face the PA.

"I'm changin' my name, Rita."

He has decided he wants to talk again.

"You're doin' what?"

"My mum said."

"Changin' your name? What do you mean?"

"I'm changin' it. Havin' a diff'rent one."

"What do you mean? Changin' Polo to somethin' else?"

"No, not my *name*."

The child is struggling to explain.

"We're both changin' it, me an' Amber."

"You're changin' your *surname*, your *family* name?"

The surprise in Rita's voice has redoubled. Polo is nodding his head.

"Pheasant!" cries little Cameron, bursting into life.

"Where's that?" asks Rita, distracted.

"What?" asks Reece who is poking around inside one of his ears.

"You must say *pardon*," Emily corrects him.

"In that field!" insists little Cameron, "In that field! I seed it!"

"I can't see one."

"I seed it, in that field!"

"It's not!" says Reece, now removing a finger from up a nostril. "You're makin'…, you're makin' it up, Cam'ron!"

In spite of the commotion behind him Polo is still in his own world.

"My mum says she's gonna change it for both of us. Me an' Amber. To Dad's name."

Rita has turned back to face him.

"You mean instead of Dale? Instead of Polo Dale?"

"Yeah."

"So, what'll your name be? What's your dad called? I might have forgot but I don't think I ever knew."

"Ashworth," he says quietly.

The argument behind them has died down.

"Ashworth? So you'll be Polo Ashworth then?"

"Yeah."

"And what do you think about that? Polo Ashworth. Do you like that name?"

"Dunno."

"You've been Polo Dale for as long as I've known you, young man."

"Don't matter."

Rita checks to see if little Cameron has settled down, if he hasn't slipped off his booster seat, if he hasn't wriggled out of his seat belt. Don gently presses on the brakes, indicating left to make the turn at the Fox & Hounds junction.

"Oh well," Rita resumes. "Polo Ashworth, then."

"It's my dad's name," says the boy tetchily. "An' he *is* my dad. An' he *is* stayin'."

There is a moment's silence, save for the noise of the mini-bus straining to climb the hill into the next village where the twins live at the outlying farm, the last pick-up before school. The mist is turning to a light drizzle. By the church a large removal van has pulled on to the flagstones, its orange warning lights flashing; the words *Dobbins of Hounslow* and a London telephone number are painted on the side. Don edges past it and spots the driver in a waterproof with his hood up striding down the lane towards a large thatched property, trying to keep the paperwork on his clipboard dry.

"Well, your mum did seem to be in a very good mood this mornin', she did," says Rita in a tone of forced cheeriness. "She must have had a long talk about it all with your dad. She must think it's a good idea."

Polo seems lost in his own thoughts for a moment, then:

"There's a pheasant! Runnin' into that hedge!"

"That's not… that's not a… not a pheasant!" demands the ever-watchful Reece. "It's a diff… a diff'rent colour."

"Course it's a pheasant, you loser! It's a female. It's a hen. You never seen a pheasant hen?"

"Polo, don't call Reece that name," says Rita. "It's not nice, and you know it's not nice."

"What-ever."

Don catches Polo's grin in his mirror.

"It's a mummy pheasant, Reece, my love. It *is* a different colour, you're right. A pale browny colour, isn't it? Not as bright as the daddy one."

From Emily's seat there is a sudden squeal:

"Weeta, look! Look!"

"What's that, my darlin'?"

"Cam'won's tooth felled out."

"What?"

"Cam'won's tooth felled out. Look!"

The little boy is on the edge of bursting into tears.

"My tooth felled out."

Rita unbuckles herself and moves to sit by him.

"You've lost a little tooth, have you, my love? Was it loose? Don't cry, Cameron. Come on, you be a big boy now. Where's it to?"

"It's there. On the floor," imparts Emily. "*Icky.*"

"That's gustin," says Polo.

"Pick it up for him, Emily, please," says Rita.

"No, it's gustin," she echoes.

Don is glancing in the mirror. Rita disappears from view then resurfaces panting, holding the tooth.

"Rita will hold on to it, Cameron. You can have it back when we stop. I'll wrap it in some tissue and you can take it home and show your mummy. She will be surprised, won't she? That's it, no cryin'. You can put it under your pillow when you go to bed and see what the tooth fairy brings in the night."

"Ain't no such thing," says Polo.

"I got a lellow one, Weeta," says Emily, from a parallel conversation.

"Beg your pardon? What do you mean, Emily?"

"A lellow one. A lellow bike."

"Oh, I see. A yellow bike. Right. That's nice. Cameron, I said *I'd* keep hold of your tooth just until we get to school. Don't cry, there's a good boy. Let's have a little song, shall we?"

Reece meanwhile has interest in neither the tooth nor the girl's bicycle. This morning his big blue eyes are forever peeled on the rolling rows of rain-soaked fields.

"Pheasant!" he shouts in triumph. "T,t,t…two of 'em!"

COUNTY HOSPITAL

I haven't seen Juliet this week, which is a pity because she is definitely my favourite. Maybe she's on holiday; she might have told me but I'm not always able to take stuff in. I shouldn't be writing this, probably. It has no place in a document authorised by the police, but maybe she'll get a pat on the back when all this is over for being such a brilliant nurse. The one I saw this morning is more buttoned-up, lacks a sense of humour; maybe she's unhappy in her life. She's rougher too, cack-handed: changing my dressings she actually hurt me and then didn't have the grace to apologise. Meanwhile the doctors are pleased with me, the physios too, but I still have days of inertia, throbbing pain, or even worse, periods of depression. They arranged for me to have sessions with a speech therapist as someone noticed certain sounds are still hard for me to form and there is often a delay from brain to tongue. As for me, I didn't notice anything untoward: I was always taught to think before opening my mouth.

What is it with human nature that we cannot remain impartial for more than five minutes? Watch a bit of telly. Read a newspaper. We cannot help ourselves. We feel sorry for unknown victims of crime, of accidents. We feel cheered by the successes of people we've never met: the sportsman, the game-show contestant, the student with her exam results, family members reunited after a lifetime apart. Their smile brings on our smile. Their laughter infects us. Their tears break our hearts. Can we watch even an obscure sporting competition between two unknowns for very long before we begin to favour, for whatever reason, one of the contestants? No matter how insular or independent we think we are, it seems there is nothing we can do to stop the arrows of empathy piercing our shields. I take my hat off to judges; they present as disinterested a view as is humanly possible, but is it really just an act, a performance of pretending to be what society expects a judge to be?

Nobody can be neutral for very long. Some of us cannot be neutral at all. Other people: we cheer them on, or we may pity them, or we despise their actions, we might smile at their foibles, we endeavour to understand them, we are heartened when they get their comeuppance. Yet we will never actually know them. The artist, the dramatist, the poet, they know this very well. They know that if we are presented with a figure, smiling or crying, deceived or deceitful, we will react. It takes us no time at all to feel contempt, sorrow, pity or perhaps respect, relief, satisfaction. We take sides. We cannot help ourselves.

So I didn't need to ask myself why it was that I was upset by the news I heard one morning on the way to school that Polo Dale was to have his surname changed to Ashworth. To have his fledgling identity molested. No matter how much he promised his family for Christmas, no matter how many times he flattered his way back into Geena Dale's affections, I could not forgive Malcolm Ashworth for leaving her to cope alone for months on end and, when the work or the women dried up in London, for coming back and feeling that he could give her a black eye whenever he got a little bit drunk or lost his temper. You see, I had taken sides. Categorically. And yet I hardly knew the family and certainly knew very little about him. I'd jumped to a conclusion and was not at all ashamed of it. Yet this wasn't a work of fiction, the act of a play that I was witnessing. This was a reality that was slowly becoming engrained into my consciousness. Not quite yet was I making *decisions* in response to the effect on my sensibilities, not at this stage was I taking *action*, but already I knew that an intuitive *reaction* within me was, like an itch, impossible to ignore.

Unlike most of the other parents of my passengers, Geena was never on the doorstep waiting for the bus with her youngest son. Some mornings she could be seen through the grubby kitchen window moving around in her dressing gown, filling a kettle, berating a child. Some mornings she was in bed and Polo had to fend for himself. But some mornings she'd be playfully pushing him out of the door at the last minute, out towards the minibus, hair springing up in all directions, red cheeked, grinning at Rita and me as she carried his bag behind him. And then she'd have a word or two, mainly with Rita, but of course I overheard: sly whispers then a burst of dirty laughter, bits of gossip about people I didn't know, complaints about her neighbours or Polo's teachers, grumbles about the price of shoes. Sometimes she would address me directly: usually a joke with a twinkle in her eye or a cheeky remark about my parking skills or my haircut or my choice of scarf. Geena is one of those people who doesn't stand on ceremony, who makes their mind up about you quickly, and if they like you (or especially if their child says he likes you) will treat you as a mate straight away. No weeks and months of getting to know you. No procrastination. What's the point? I liked that in her. And she was at this time, towards the end of that first autumn term, in a breezy mood more often than not. So, give him his due, Malcolm must have been doing something right.

I didn't see much of Polo's father, even when he was in the middle of a residential at The Pavilions. Now and again it must have been his turn to bring the boy out to the bus, reminding him to behave himself in class and giving him a showy squeeze. And then at the end of the day, if Geena was at work, he would come traipsing out of the house, disturbed by the beep-beep of my horn, looking like he'd been in the middle of a particularly draining nap. He'd light up a cigarette, appear at the door and give me a perfunctory nod. As Polo stepped off the bus, Ashworth would ask him if he'd been good (for our benefit?), and the boy would shrug and scurry past him into the kitchen. In my limited experience of their interaction, I never heard him address Polo by his name; as if to reinforce a wobbly concept, it was always "son".

On other afternoons Polo's older brother Angelo might appear at the kitchen window with a functional wave of acknowledgement. We are not allowed to leave a child at an address without an adult confirming a transfer of responsibility. Angelo never has much to say: he is a scowler in an NY baseball cap. The fall-back was Geena's neighbour at No.3, whose own front was littered with large plastic toys left outside in all weathers to grow discoloured and rusty. I have no recollection of her name, if ever I was told it. She is about the same age as Geena but looks younger. She dresses like a stringy teenager, and her gaunt face, framed in a mop of lank hair, is pierced in places with studs and rings and pins. I don't think Polo is too fond of her, but the arrangement is in place and, being unemployed and without transport, she is reliably and unswervingly on site. She and Geena fall out regularly, Rita told me, but she never lets the children down. Geena accused her once of stealing a bottle of vodka from her kitchen and didn't speak to her for a week; then Geena herself was accused of snogging the woman's boyfriend and the cold war lasted a fortnight. Both accusations were based, apparently, on fact. Usually, if she were in the mood, she would exchange a few words with me rather than with Rita. She'd saunter up to the bus and I'd be obliged to wind down the window. I didn't look forward to these brief encounters; with her stary eyes, her broken front tooth and breath that reeked of cider, the woman frankly gave me the creeps.

Polo was still missing school from time to time; a tummy bug, a sore throat or often for no other reason than the family oversleeping. Geena would sometimes appear at the door in her flimsy dressing gown, flustered and self-re-proaching: the alarm hadn't gone off (*sorry, Reet!*) but she promised to drive him into school later. She rarely did. More than once we arrived and the house would be silent, curtains closed, no sign of life. We would leave without him. We had no choice. If Polo was genuinely ill we only heard about it when we reached the house. It was Rita's only gripe that Geena never rang her at home in time so we wouldn't have to make the detour through her village for nothing. She'd say she'd lost her number or even *misplaced* her phone. Rita didn't believe her for one second, but the next morning, if she saw her striding towards the bus with her daft smile, Polo's lunchbox and a funny story about her run-in with the silly bitch at the post office, she couldn't help but instantly forgive her.

As for the boy, he didn't seem to mind the extra days off. He didn't enjoy school, but I could see that he was bright and was missing a trick. He was well behind with reading and writing, but he was a lively talker with good vocabulary when he was in the mood, and he could deal pretty readily with numbers. Sometimes he chose to sit directly behind me and I used to give him arithmetical puzzles to solve as we drove along: if ten farmers had ten tractors and six of them broke down... that kind of thing. I wished he'd make a better job of cleaning his teeth, but it wasn't my place to start making suggestions like that.

He still used Gabe's old earphones now and again if he remembered to charge up his PlayStation. I was pleased that he hadn't broken or lost them. Sometimes he brought a magazine to read on the bus: something his dad had bought him - cars or football. Not angling: his dad wasn't interested. One day I asked him which football team he supported. He said Chelsea. I ribbed him that Chelsea were rubbish. Indignantly he maintained that they were the best team in the league and had all the best players. But when

I asked him who his favourite Chelsea footballer was, he could only name a player who had left the club almost two years earlier.

SEVEN

The scene plays in the same police station. It appears to be evening or one of those dismal days in March before the clocks go forward and the late afternoon gloom makes it feel like midnight. The room is large, a nondescript work space, almost empty of people. Don is sitting at a cluttered work station reading what looks like a single page letter by the yellow glow of a desk-lamp. Soft footsteps approach him from behind and a hand is placed on his shoulder; it is Paul Tufts, dressed in an unbuttoned coat and scarf, ready to leave the building.

"Sorry to disturb you, Don," he says quietly.

Don turns in his seat and offers his colleague a tired smile.

"Oh, it's you. I was miles away."

"Fancy coming up to the pool for a swim?" asks the younger man. "I'm just off there now. Bit of exercise? Get the heart pumping again?"

"Thanks, Paul. I don't think I'm really in the mood tonight."

"It'd do you good."

"Maybe."

"What's up?"

"Nothing. Just don't fancy it. Thanks for asking."

Tufts looks distractedly at a notice board on the far wall.

"I've just come down from seeing Coppinger," he says presently. "He told me you are planning to leave us. Retiring early."

"Yeah. That's right. I am."

"Well, I'm surprised. And sorry."

"Sorry?"

"Yes. Absolutely."

Don takes a deep breath and sighs.

"I've been thinking about it for a while now," he says. "I'm fifty-two."

"That's no age for a detective."

"Maybe not."

"Well then?"

"It's been becoming a chore, Paul. I've been getting less and less pleasure out of the job lately. Well, for a couple of years, really. I've had enough, basically."

The other man is not inclined to interrupt. Don chugs on:

"The career structure has never really worked for me. Not in this division. And I don't want to move out of the area. If I carried on it would just be more of the same until age really did catch up with me."

Tufts looks concerned, as if he is somehow personally responsible.

"What'll you do?"

"No idea at present."

"You'll need something."

"I can take my pension. Find something part-time, maybe. I just need a break first. Headspace, I think they call it."

"You're worn out."

"Jaded is the word." Don smiles.

"It's a damn shame. You're a good cop, Don. We can't afford to lose people like you."

"Well, everyone's replaceable."

"I don't know about that."

There is a moment's silence. Don turns back to the letter that is still in his hand. Tufts leans forward a little to look over his shoulder.

"What are you doing, old man? Composing your farewell speech?"

"This? No, this is a letter that came this morning. Can you believe that? In this age of emails and text messages? Somebody actually sat down and wrote me a letter and put it in an envelope with a stamp on."

Tufts is smiling.

"Is it important?"

"Doubtful. Not important beyond him and me. It's from Kermit's father. I thought he was back in Poland. He says he saw me at the funeral. I didn't notice him though. He must have kept a very low profile and left before the end."

"May I?"

Don passes over the paper.

"Be my guest."

And as Don begins to tidy his desk, DS Tufts reads the note: good quality white paper, handwritten words in black ink, a heavy foreign script; dated yesterday, no address.

Don knows exactly what Tufts is reading. Having read it over ten times or more, he knows the text word for word:

Mister Donnal Percey,

I thank you for coming to the funeral of my boy. I seen you from a distance. I know your face of course. Tomasz has speak to me often about you, you know. We know how you police treat him. I must thank you for every thing you police have done for Tomasz. It is possible the boy rest in peace now, I think, far from this place which was never fair to him.

Do not worry, Mr Percey. I will repay you one day. If it is possible. I make it a vow for the memory of my son.

Kremitz

Just as Tufts is reaching the end, Don stands, stretches over and flicks off his desk lamp, and suddenly the image is lost.

They sent a young detective constable on an errand today to take away what I have been writing in the last week or so. They do that from time to time, just about as erratically as I am managing to produce new material for them. Sometimes they send somebody here and then they are disappointed to discover that I've written nothing at all since their last visit. Some days I feel too lethargic to write. Other days my mind is like an empty cupboard. I blame the medication, which I think they are changing day by day. I overheard Gabe talking to Dr Pickering about it but I have no recollection of anything they said.

She left me the laptop, obviously. She just retrieved the stuff with a memory stick, smiled and left me to doze. I lie back and watch as the electronics work their silent magic. I feel like you do when you give blood.

Actually she did speak to me a little. She must have been told to ask me a couple of questions. The same question twice, really: *Could I remember being threatened? Had I ever been intimidated?* At the time I was barely awake. When her enquiries registered I had little energy to think of an answer and I must have simply shaken my head.

Of course there have been occasions when some villain has threatened to come after me but that's in the distant past. I think she meant more recently, since I left the police force.

Now my mind is clearer I can remember one incident which did freak me out, just at the turn of the year, in the dead of winter. One evening, quite late, I was at home alone, obviously, in a bit of a stupor, thinking about calling it a night, half-watching something drab on the television. The logs in the wood stove had all but burnt out and as I was in the habit of watching TV with just a small lamp on, the room was dark, full of shadows. All of a sudden, over the sound of the programme, I heard what I thought was the crack of a tree branch out in the garden. I was alarmed because it was not a windy night. A moment later I heard the noise of somebody or some animal shuffling about in the darkness outside, just beyond the French windows. I muted the TV and sat rigid, listening harder for sounds through the curtains: nothing for several seconds, then the scratching of boots on gravel. It was hard to tell just how close to the house the movement was. I stood and slowly approached the windows, eyes and ears alert for disturbance. Someone was outside, I knew, creeping around in the dark. But how many of them? I could feel my heart picking up speed.

At the exact moment I drew back the curtains there was a brittle roar of an engine and a pair of headlights dazzled me with the white glow of their full beam. For anyone watching from behind me, it would have been like the scene from the film *Close Encounters*. I reeled backwards, caught my balance and, shielding my eyes, opened the windows and stepped into the garden. Once out of the direct glare I could see an oversized quad-bike being manoeuvred into the space of the neighbour's hangar.

What the hell are you doing at this time of night? I must have shouted. Something like that. I thought Otterbridge hadn't heard me at first, but he cut the engine and called back through the night air: *I'm moving my new toy into my garage. What does it look like I'm doing? It's not a fucking crime, is it, officer?*

I have been thinking further about the detective's question.

The memory of an unexpected letter I received in my last days as a copper flashed back to me. It was a letter from

Tadeusz Kremitz, Kermit's father, posted in London, which arrived not long after the boy's funeral. I still think of him as a boy, even though he was nearly twenty-one when he died. I had not spotted the father at the crematorium, but did exchange a few words with the mother who made an effort to be pleasant. She introduced me to her partner, the boat-yard owner, a bony-faced rake of a man whom I mistook at first for one of the undertaker's men and who had little inclination to make eye contact. Tadeusz must have observed the mourners from the shadows like some spy operating behind enemy lines.

I can recall the contents of his letter quite clearly even now, as it was succinct and boldly written in a hand that was distinct, striking even. On the face of it it was a letter of thanks for everything I, we, the police had done for his son. At the close of it he wrote that he vowed to repay us, repay me. Did he mean me personally? Was he expressing genuine gratitude or something more sinister?

I don't know the man well enough to tell if he was making a promise or issuing a threat. Do I remember feeling *intimidated*, the word the detective used? Not exactly, perhaps, but the letter puzzled me, disquieted me, haunted me for days.

EIGHT

The scene plays in a familiar room in a familiar home. A heavy shower of summer rain is beating against the window of a sort of office, a study with a large mahogany writing desk, a matching pair of bookcases and a filing cabinet. The walls are decorated with framed photographs, vivid prints and a calendar, all representative of colourful aspects of Indian culture. Sitting at the desk in a sturdy part-upholstered seat is Don Percey, casually dressed, not long retired, refreshed from having severed the ties that had bound him to the duties of the county constabulary for thirty years and more.

Before him sits the large family iMac, its sleek keyboard home to his fingertips, its screen flickering from one sharp image to the next, casting its pale glow over his features. It was Carole's choice of computer. It has taken him an age to find the password to her account and this morning Don has finally forced himself to sift through his wife's endless queue of emails: inbox, sent, drafts, everything he can readily find, just in case there is something important he has missed in their joint policies, in the documentation of their shared life.

And, taken by surprise, he has tripped head first into a correspondence between his wife and a colleague of hers which is evolving into something a little more private, a little more tender than he could have expected.

Don's face is already turning a little bloodless, his heart

seems to have stopped beating, and his expression hardens as his dead eyes scan and rescan first one and then a second of two e-mails that he wishes he had never found. He nervously taps from one to the other and his heart is pounding again, the blood racing to his cheekbones; one minute he's in a shiver, the next he can feel body heat drifting up from his open shirt. The rain is whipping more fiercely than ever against the panes. Baiting him, the e-mails refuse to disappear. Wanting to believe in their innocence, he tries hopelessly not to read between the lines:

MARCH 26th

TO: Carole Percey

FROM: Robledo, Graeme<g.robledo14@beemail.com>

SUBJECT: St Christopher's

Carole,

Delighted that you'll be working on my team again after Easter. We need somebody with a sense of humour - and who is definitely on my wavelength! I'll be back in touch during the holidays, but in the meantime I'm attaching some preliminaries re. St Christopher's. As you know, it's a full five days - they've been in special measures, but the vibes are positive. At least one gets to meet some nice people on this job.

Let me know if you need any clarification.

As I say, I'll speak to you before we meet. Looking forward to it - the school is in a dreary part of the country, so I hope they can find us all a nice cosy hotel!

Fondly,

Graeme

MAY 13th

TO: *Carole Percey*

FROM: *Robledo, Graeme<g.robledo14@beemail.com>*

SUBJECT: Brydmouth Hall

Dear Carole,

Thanks again for all your valued input to the St Christopher's inspection. I've just about completed the final report. It'll be published next week.

You know you said you were looking to change jobs? And I told you I thought that my replacement at Brydmouth Hall might be leaving? Well, inside track, she is definitely leaving, probably in the autumn. Having to move back north for family reasons. Anyway, I've attached some stuff I wrote about the school, plus the link to their new website. It's a lovely school, Carole - you'd be perfect for it! Have a look. I'm sure I could talk to a few people for you.

We can chat about it all in London next month. I assume you are still planning to be at the conference? I do hope so. I look forward so much to spending a little more time in your company.

Fondest,

Graeme

COUNTY HOSPITAL

September

Juliet mentioned that the school holidays are already over. I had lost track of the weeks passing but I do remember Gabriel telling me some time ago that Oliver was getting excited about starting in a new class soon.

I have been wondering who will be driving the minibus this term in my place; I'm sure John will have worked something out. Rita called in to spend half an hour with me a few days ago. She looked well, had a nice tan, a new hairstyle. A summer cut, she said. She'd been to Majorca for a fortnight with her husband and her daughter's family. She showed me some photos. As she left I made her promise that she would give my love to the children on the bus.

The laptop has reappeared but it has been missing for a day or two. I'm not sure why. Nobody seems to know the reason but perhaps they're just not saying. Were they imposing a break on me? I probably needed it, to be honest. I have been going at it full throttle. Plus, I'm talking better. More coherently. Making more sense. Pickering is pleased with me. A very professional man, I'd say. Old-fashioned, in a good way. Polite. Sincere. There, Doctor, there's a nice name check for you. He'll give the police full access, unlimited time with me soon, I should think. But now I've started, I'm going to finish this document anyway, right to the end, wherever the end is. It's doing me good. I'm enjoying the excitement of rediscovering where I've been.

I've been thinking about my wife. She keeps reappearing in my thoughts. I should say my ex-wife. No, that's wrong. My late wife. My dead wife. Carole. The wife who died in the accident. A year ago? At least one year. I can't quite remember. I don't think she's related to what happened to me, to why I am in this hospital bed, still here after all these weeks, but I can't be sure. *Write what you want,* they said. *Let your mind wander, write it all down, whether you think it's important or not. Let us be the judges of that, Don.*

She keeps reappearing in my thoughts.

Carole and I were married for over thirty years. Not exactly smooth sailing, I admit, but we had more ups than downs, and for most of that time we were in love. I suppose there's a time in every marriage when the buzz becomes a drone. We met at her first school. She'd been teaching there just about a year when there was a break-in one night and I was one of the officers assigned to the tidy-up. I remember talking to her - her classroom window was the one that had been breached. *She* was a bit nervous because I was a big strapping policeman, and *I* was a bit nervous because she was simply gorgeous.

We had only a little in common at the time, but I suppose a sexual attraction goes a long way. We explored the countryside together, cycling or on foot. I showed her a part of England she was still fairly new to, walking for miles across the county's chalky uplands, along its ridgeways, tramping through woods of beech and oak and ash, and down on to the coast we skirted cliff tops and pine-edged bays. Carole was a city girl at heart but she came to love her new surroundings.

What else brought us together? One, we both enjoyed Indian food. Two, on more than one occasion I repaired her little white Renault 5. Three, she understood cricket (her father had played to a decent level) and I could have as rewarding a conversation about it with her as with any colleague down at the station. In my playing days with both the police and the village team she used to turn up and sit in the sunshine to watch for an hour, longer if I was batting. Never too long, though; I was an impulsive batsman and was easy to tempt into swinging at a wide delivery. Caught out every time. Too impatient. But if I had played well she'd hug me with her cheeks aglow, her eyes alight with pride. It was a time when the lemonade always had a fizz and there was not a thought to it ever going flat.

Gradually we could share a love of books, especially poetry. As a student of literature (BA in English Lit, UCL), Carole had taken the scenic mountain route via Shakespeare and Browning, whereas I had self-consciously scuttered away along the starlit side streets of Dylan and Springsteen. She became my tutor and I her eager pupil, enchanted by the sparkle of Oberon and Puck, delighted by the zest of Lear's Fool. As a birthday treat she took me to the theatre in London for the first time in my life. And in return I suppose I was her protector. *My big, burly, heroic teddy bear.* Her words. *After a day at school,* she said, *there's nothing I like better than falling into your lovely big strong arms.*

Gabriel was born very soon. Perhaps too soon. Later we tried for a second child but without success. Things became complicated and a little bitter. During Carole's career break, her *nappy years*, as she called them, I was taking on overtime and studying for a move out of uniform. She was very keen for me to progress. I know she was more disappointed than I was that my police career stalled less than halfway up the ladder.

As if to compensate, to guarantee our financial independence, Carole was determined to get on in education. She moved on twice, hopping to a deputy head's job in the town's largest primary and then to the head teacher's post in our own village school. Success emboldened her ambition. She rose to the top of her pay scale and took on the responsibility of advising certain committees at County Hall. She was seconded for a term to another school to support a head teacher who was losing his grip. And in the last years before her death she had extended her energies into school inspections, working intermittently for Ofsted on teams visiting establishments far beyond the county. *At least one of us will be an inspector now*, she quipped as she read the letter confirming her place on a preliminary course, but it was a pointed joke which came from behind dull eyes.

The education of our own son was a sore point, but one which I was prepared to concede before it left a scar. We have a perfectly good school in town, Green Bank: an 11-18 co-educational comprehensive (*good with outstanding features*, latest Ofsted report, and no worse to my mind back when Gabe was on the point of moving there). Carole, however, had got it into her head that the boy would not be stretched there. She knew some disturbing things about Green Bank, she said, and behind my back had done some considerable research into alternatives. Although she was a product of, and now a contributor to the state education system, I had noticed hints dropped about the greater opportunities in the private sector, not only in respect of perceived academic standards but also in the chance to mix with the *fragrant classes*. Her words. I was angry and dug my heels in. Well, up to a point. Only up to a point. At the age of eleven Gabe was wearing the royal blue blazer of the independent grammar school in the county town.

My decision to quit the police force came after months if not years of erosion. Carole knew how depressed I got and, yes, she was sympathetic, comforting, supportive. There had been days, of course, when I had been a shoulder for *her* to cry on. Nevertheless, I think that she always believed that I would battle on, my gaze still locked on that next rung, bringing home the steady salary until I was somewhere near sixty. She suggested I took a year off and then went back to the force. Or get a transfer. Or ask for a job in admin. Had she really understood me? Had she really been listening? It wasn't the sudden decline in our income that concerned her in the end, but rather her own disappointment in my inability or, even worse, my unwillingness to carry on as a detective sergeant. More than disappointment I sensed a disdain, unspoken but awakened. Her mouth had uttered the right words of support and solidarity, but her cold eyes spoke of a new reality in which she was forging ahead with a significant career and I was nowhere. No backbone, washed out, an empty shell. She said she still loved me, and we joked about a change to our shopping and cooking schedules, but silently, secretly, she could no longer respect me in quite the same way.

And then, in recent times, to what extent was Carole's attraction to private education being revived? Much of this period remains in a mist for me just now, but I do remember something of the aftermath of Carole's death. I remember the brutal finality of her funeral. I remember the desolation of staring into her wardrobe of defunct clothes, finding insignificant things in cupboards and drawers, things that she had bought for the future, things like boxes of French soap and special candles for Christmas and birthday cards she would now never write. Even the sight of her favourite coffee mug sitting rinsed and dried next to mine on the kitchen shelf cored me like an apple.

I remember tidying up her *affairs,* her life's loose strings running untied and wild. And I remember something she said to me on the night before she went on that conference trip to London. *Don, we need to have a proper talk when I get back. There's something I need to tell you*. She refused to expand on this. She told me not to worry. She was too busy that evening. She had too much else to think about. Then the phone kept ringing. Then a neighbour called round for a favour. The moment was lost. *A proper talk when I get back.*

I have never met Graeme Robledo. But I have read his e-mails. At least the ones he wrote to Carole. *Fondly. Fondest.* I went into her inbox a few days after she died - for innocent reasons. Most of her correspondents were only vaguely familiar at best: work colleagues mainly. I glanced at them all, vainly searching for any clue as to why my wife had been ripped out of my life, but it seems as though we are all to remain literally clueless as to the absurdity, the randomness of this fragile existence. Graeme Robledo was one of many people who e-mailed her; in his case the messages began quite recently, no more than a few months before. One of them stands out in my mind, especially now. He wrote to Carole to encourage her to apply for a job in a prep school a hundred miles from her home. From *our* home.

Brydmouth Hall. I remember the name. I looked it up on the internet. Very smart, very fragrant. The school was an eighteenth-century manor house converted and extended into its wooded grounds, which sloped gracefully down to the estuary where privileged young boys and girls could learn to sail. I read the head teacher's mission statement and studied her warm, intelligent face in the photograph where she was sitting diligently in her study. On the wall behind her was the school crest with its silver trident on a navy blue shield. I examined the online prospectus and saw crisp photographs of shiny-faced, lustrous-haired children smiling knowingly at the camera as if in self-congratulation as to their good fortune. Boys in navy and white hoops were playing rugby, girls were stroking ponies, novice sailors were having fun in dinghies. Children were pretending to play peek-a-boo behind a handsome oak. From within these glossy portraits I could almost hear the ski holiday chatter, the mock-adult discussion of the merits of Daddy's new Jag.

And in a news-page gallery I even found Carole's erudite patron.

A round, rosy-faced figure, he was pictured with two other worthies, each clutching a glass of wine. His smile, framed by a neat grey beard, was genuine but his eyes were aimed beyond the camera. He looked distracted or perhaps slightly drunk. He was captioned as *our former Head teacher Mr Graeme Robledo-Brown MA, DPhil, a most welcome visitor to the school for the centenary celebrations.* I guessed that he had since become a full-time lead inspector of schools and, in the meantime, an enthusiast for Carole: a supporter, an admirer, her champion, to say the very least.

NINE

The scene plays by the same minibus, parked outside No.1 The Pavilions. It is an ice-clear winter's morning, a blood orange sun sits low in an empty sky, a silver frosting lies over the grass in front of the house blocks. Don is sitting in his driver's seat, half-listening to someone else's conversation, fidgeting, playing with his discarded scarf, impatient to drive on. Geena Dale wants to talk forever, no matter that it's perishing out there. And Rita won't stop her. They're alright for time, as it happens: no need to pick up Cameron today, he's got a hospital appointment. The heater has been on maximum for over half an hour and just as the bus was starting to warm up, now the sliding door is wide open and the heat is dissipating into the bitter air.

Geena's voice fills the space. She is standing in her pyjamas and dressing gown, gesticulating with her hands. Her wrists are bare, red from chafing, left and right. One foot rests on the bus-step, both feet in matching slippers but unmatched socks, and covering most of her unbrushed hair is a sloppy woolly hat.

"No, Mal's gone. He buggered off yesterday. When I came home he's taken all his stuff, and, listen to this, Reet, he'd made off with the telly. We'd had a big row."

"He took your TV?"

"Yeah. Forty-two inch. Well, *he* bought it. He threatened he'd take it. Said it was his by rights. Even though it's been at this house for the past three years or more. Now we don't have one makes no difference to him. Angelo's well pissed off with him."

She lowers her voice but Don can still hear.

"He's a bastard, Reet. I don't know why I let him stay here again. I'm too soft, that's my trouble. Too bloody soft. Anyway, he's burnt his bridges now. That's him finished. He's gone and good fuckin' riddance."

Rita raises an eyebrow and tilts her head towards the children.

"Sorry, sorry, sorry," whispers Geena, suitably admonished. "I must keep my voice down."

"So, where's he gone then?"

"I dunno. London, I suppose. He'd been talkin' about there bein' some shop-fittin' work, but that was supposed to be after Christmas."

"Well, I'm sorry for you, Geena, love."

"Don't be. I'm happy he's gone."

"You seemed to be happy havin' him around these past weeks."

"Yeah, well. I was an idiot. Puttin' up with him. His drinkin'. His ways. He's an idle sod, Reet. Don't lift a finger in the kitchen. Won't help or nothin'. Slaps the kids when he's in a mood. Good riddance, yeah? I'm better off without him."

Rita holds back her counsel, which is tacit agreement in itself. Don coughs theatrically to remind her she's on a bus, at work, on duty, not in a gossipy corner of a café, but she's looking away, back into the bus where Polo is plugging in his earphones.

"And how's Polo taken it?" she asks under her breath.

"He was cryin' a bit last night," says Geena rubbing her hands together, finally beginning to notice the temperature. "What you would expect. He is his dad an' all. An' Amber. She's upset too. Don't want to go to school this mornin'. But they'll come round. We've been without him before, ain't we? We're used to it. This time is it, though, Reet. Finished. I'll not be havin' him back."

"He seems okay now," says Rita, watching the boy fastening his seat belt without being reminded. "A bit quiet, but…"

"Polo's more upset about the bloody telly than anythin' else!" says Geena with a throaty laugh. "I must get him somethin' to take his mind off it. Somethin' nice. A little treat."

"Well, it'll be Christmas soon."

Don is looking round to the seats behind him.

"We'd better be going, don't you think, ladies?" he suggests.

"Yeah, the kids are excited already," Geena goes on as if she hasn't heard him at all. "I'll make sure we have a nice Christmas, don't you worry. I'd do anythin' for my kids, you know that, Reet. Well, within reason." A hollow smile escapes. "But I'm not sure how. I'm just about keepin' my head above water. I've asked for more hours, but they can't promise. I might have to borrow."

"Oh, don't go down that road, Geena. Those loan sharks, you'll never get rid once you start."

"No, I suppose. But it's an expensive time, ain't it, Christmas?"

"You'll have to cut out the ciggies," says Rita, trying to lighten the mood. "Just think how much…"

"Oh, I have! I have already."

Rita is edging towards the door. Don has wrapped his scarf

around his neck again. Geena realises she is stretching the truth about the cigarettes.

"Well, I'm tryin'," she says laughing again, this time at herself. "I'm tryin' my best. None today yet. An' another thing – sorry, Don, just let me finish – looks like I need a new washin' machine. Bloody thing's playin' up, makin' funny noises, scrapin' noises. Don't sound too clever at all. I dunno. I reckon Mal's buggered it up. Blame him anyway. Oh, I dunno, we'll sort it out. We'll sort ourselves out, won't we, Polo? He's not listenin'; got his music on. Listen, I'm keepin' you from getting' on your way. Sorry, Don. Don looks like he's had enough of me goin' on. Sorry, Don, we're just talkin'! Anyway, I'm goin' indoors. It's freezin' out here. Got to get Amber's breakfast ready anyway. Sorry! I'll see you later, Reet. I'll be back in time this afternoon. See you then, yeah?

"Bye, Don! Bye, Polo, my love. Be good! Mummy's angel!"

Rita slams the door, Don revs the engine, and Geena blows exaggerated kisses to her son through the window.

COUNTY HOSPITAL

When Polo Dale was excluded from school for three days it was a shock but hardly a surprise. He'd been sent home before (I don't think Geena was too pleased to have to drive herself in to go and collect him mid-morning), but this time the punishment followed a longer consultation with the head teacher. Three days off just before the Christmas holidays wouldn't be such a hardship for him, you might think, but he was genuinely upset, I believe, and especially bitter about missing the Christmas party. Of course, it was entirely his own fault. His mother admitted he'd been *a bit depressed*, and after an ill-tempered morning and a dressing-down from his class teacher, the boy had shattered a pair of staffroom windows with a rounders bat during playtime. I think he spent most of his exclusion time down by the river on his own with a home-made rod and line looking for stickleback until it got too cold for him to sit still. Whatever, we didn't have to make the stop at his village until the following week.

All this was shortly after Malcolm Ashworth's sudden departure from the family home, and the fractious manner of his disappearance was no doubt, if not an excuse, then at least the mood music for Polo's antisocial behaviour. Geena was angry with the school at first. She spoke to both Rita and me about one of the *bitch teachers* who *always had it in for him.* Then her anger again turned towards the absent father. *He screws up the boy's head.* Then she blamed herself. And finally she turned on the boy. It was an unpleasant interlude, but quickly passed. Polo returned to school, reluctantly and yet with a brazen face, in time for the final days of term.

The children on the bus were wildly excited about Christmas. They had been singing fragments of off-key carols since the middle of November. They'd already had a couple of days of snow, which had closed the school, and now they were praying for more. Rita was in the habit of buying each one of them a selection box and giving a card to them and their parents. I was happy to offer to go along with that, signing the cards and making a donation to her outlay on the chocolate. By the time she had presented Polo with the seasonally wrapped but poorly disguised Christmas gift, a cheeky smile had returned to his face. I admit I broke any code of equality by surreptitiously adding to his presents. Well, Rita knew, but the other children were unaware. It was nothing much, but I had looked out an old book on British rivers for him which I knew Gabe had left somewhere in the attic; old but in excellent condition - as good as new, really. And I splashed out £10 on a Chelsea FC calendar: twelve colour pictures of current players for the boy to follow.

Rita had mentioned to me that we were likely to be given little gifts in return from the grateful parents of some of our daily passengers. And, as she predicted, the offerings were inconsistent, varying in monetary value according to either the household income or the generosity of the donor, and ranging from a bottle of sparkling wine (from Cameron's parents, both doctors) to nothing at all. That Geena Dale, for all her money worries, should present us each with a box of fudge on our final afternoon of the term with a most genuine smile on her face - *It looks like snow, and we're going to have a whale of a time!* - touched me deeply. I was surprised that the image of her scurrying back into her house, right hand still aloft waving us goodbye, left hand encumbered by Polo's lunchbox and coat, pretending to chase her son through the door, this image stayed with me for many days, well into the Christmas period.

I spent Christmas Day with Gabriel and Grace and Oliver at their overheated home. Is it churlish of me to comment that it was a day of excess? There were too many presents for a six-year-old (but who could begrudge him wallowing in his treasure?), too much food, too many longueurs. It was the first Christmas since Carole had died and I missed her more than ever. It was a rare white one and she would have loved tramping out in her boots in the snow. One year we spent a couple of days in between Boxing Day and New Year's Eve in Wales: a tiny B&B in the Brecon Beacons where it had snowed heavily on the day we arrived. Mr & Mrs Pritchard's: a cold bed but a splendid breakfast. Gabe must have been one year old at the most; I remember carrying him in a kind of back-pack up and down mountains of pure white, stopping from time to time for a cup of coffee from Carole's Thermos, an impromptu snowball fight, a kiss and a squeeze, a moment to catch our breath and admire the view. We thought we were in Switzerland. *This is better than the Alps*, Carole said. *When you get back down the mountain here you can have a proper cup of tea and a bacon sandwich.*

She loved Christmas, everything about it. She loved the sparkle that danced in people's eyes, the rosy glow it put on people's cheeks, the music, the energy, the joy it could bring to people's spirits. And this joy had been multiplied for her since Oliver had been born, and now he was old enough to appreciate it all for himself. He would have many more days like this, unforgettable, excitable, joyful days all through his childhood, well into his teens, and Carole would miss them all. She's no longer here to see his face light up to discover what Santa has left underneath the tree. She's no longer here to see his smile, to hear his giggles, to caress his soft hair and kiss him goodnight.

Alone on the sofa with an oversized glass of whisky, I felt like a spare part, and if she'd been there with me, at least we could have laughed about being a couple of spare parts together. I even wished, absurdly, that I had invited Geena and Polo and Amber round for the day. I was quietly relieved that Malcolm was no longer a part of the family. I daydreamed about how Geena might make an effort to dress up for the occasion. I imagined her with her hair tidied up, in a nice new dress and a splash of perfume, a pair of daft Christmas earrings on, and a gin and tonic in her hand: she would be making us all laugh with a rambling tale of some clown in her village or complimenting Grace on her choice of new kitchen appliances. Gabe and Polo were sprawled on the long sofa, excitedly playing the latest FIFA game on Gabe's new Xbox, while Oliver and Amber would be sitting behind it sharing a secret bar of chocolate, heads together, reading from a colourful picture-book. Of course it was nonsense, an idle fantasy. I'd had a bit to drink. To tell the truth I was embarrassed that the notion had even crossed my mind.

Polo never got his BMX, by the way.

Much of the snow lingered into the dying days of December. Frosty nights were bitter and relentless until the New Year, which arrived apologetically and whose damp, grey January days followed one after the other like a long sequence of losing lottery tickets.

The next time I saw Geena Dale she had changed the colour of her hair to a sandy brown. I don't know if it was her natural colour, but I thought it suited her better. I said nothing. She seemed preoccupied and uttered only a few words, mostly addressed *sotto voce* to Rita as Polo settled into his seat. She appeared to be relaxed, in control: she was dressed, maybe for work, the boy was as smart as I'd ever seen him and he had a full lunchbox. Was this a resolution for the new year? Whatever, it lasted only two days,

I remember, for on the Wednesday nobody came to meet the bus, the curtains were closed and we had to drive off without him.

On some mornings she was in her pyjamas, and on others we'd arrive and little Amber would be on her own at the open door in just a pair of knickers (in January!), drinking from a carton of milk. Even if Angelo was staying with them he was never up and about at eight o'clock. Polo could never find his shoes. One morning Geena was in a panic as she had missed the alarm and, calling from inside the front door in her shabby dressing gown, she begged me to wait five minutes while she got Polo ready. As she stooped to pick out a shoe from under a low table in the hallway, her dressing gown fell open and I could not avoid the briefest glimpse of the curves of her white breast and a bare pink nipple, bristled in the cold air. She lifted the shoe and pulled the wings of the garment together in one light movement. It happened so quickly that nobody noticed the direction of my gaze. I could have looked away but I did not. It was as instinctive as the faint tingle of electricity in my groin. I heard Rita muttering that if we had to wait five minutes at every pick-up we'd never get to school on time.

I don't remember very much about the spring term. The job was becoming a little humdrum, to be honest. The days grew longer and the afternoon sun, gaining strength, arced higher in the sky like a young buzzard. Milky snowdrops gave way to wild buttoned primroses beneath the hedgerows, and the hawthorn budded and blossomed white, framing muddy, bleak winter fields which in turn slowly revealed their studded patterns of fresh green shoots through the morning mists. The children's game of Spot the Pheasant gave way to Spot the Tractor. Polo joined in less frequently. He was already beginning to behave as though he was too mature for silly childish games. He would have his eleventh birthday before too long and was already thinking about his move to the Big School after the summer; a move, I could tell, that both excited and scared him.

He wasn't too old for tears, though. One morning I thought I saw him sobbing quietly as he got on the bus. His mother was nowhere to be seen. Rita said something to him and he seemed to recover. When we arrived at school and she took charge of the little ones as usual like a fussy tour guide, Polo hung back and asked me to walk into the building with him. He was on the verge of crying once again, I could see, and I asked him what the matter was. *I ain't had no breakfast,* he whispered, the tears fell and he clung to me for support. He actually wanted me to hug him back, to hold him, to comfort him, just for a few seconds. I was aware that touching the children is a minefield but I had no choice. Just for a few seconds, and then he sniffed, took a deep breath and walked off across the playground before any of his classmates saw him in distress. On the way home that afternoon he was fine, as bubbly and boyish and mischievous as ever.

Sometime early on in the new term I remember asking Polo who was the footballer on the January page of his calendar. He was in a bad mood, I recall, and I should have saved my question for later. He pretended he hadn't heard me. When we stopped at traffic lights I turned round to ask him again. This time his answer was clear: *I dunno,* he said, *I hide it in my drawer now. Angelo ripped up the January one 'cos he said that player was a pile of shit.*

TEN

The scene plays in a familiar room in a familiar home. The only sound is that of three lean rashers of bacon sputtering in a frying pan which seems too large for them. Don has already taken the ketchup from the fridge and is quietly buttering two thick slices of plain white bread, the sort that Carole would never have bought. Suddenly, through the open kitchen window, he hears purposeful footsteps on the drive, then a little squeak and a slap as a handful of mail lands on the mat in the hallway. The footsteps recede as the bacon sizzles to a crisp. Don turns off the gas. It's a new postman these days; the old one retired, he thinks, or was reassigned or made redundant in the wake of privatisation.

Don is now in the hall, sitting at the foot of the stairs, on the oatmeal carpet that could do with a vac, fingering through the post. There has been plenty of post for him lately, for both of them, in fact, although Carole is no longer here to read hers: stuff from banks, solicitors, telephone companies. Today it's mostly junk mail, but in amongst it all a cream-coloured envelope catches his eye: their address neatly handwritten, a first-class stamp, postmarked yesterday, London NW8.

And now Don is back in the kitchen, his sandwich still unmade, sitting at the table with the envelope sliced open with the breadknife, reading and re-reading the words on the matching cream paper:

St John's Wood

18 June

My dear Donald,

I know this letter will find you still distraught over the death of your darling Carole. I regret I can add so little to the words we shared on the telephone last week to help to ease your pain.

I wanted to enclose a few sentences with the card firstly to repeat my feelings of deepest sympathy and secondly to wish you luck in your attempts to chase the scaffolding company over the legal hurdles to obtain the just amount of compensation. As far as I can see, it is a clear case of negligence and, as I said, I cannot imagine any obstruction on their part. Not that any monetary sum will ever compensate for your loss.

I knew Carole for less than one year, but in that short time she had become not only a valued and insightful member of my team but also a dear personal friend whom I shall miss terribly. I loved her warmth, her vitality, and how her eyes could sparkle with both mischief and delight. You must have seen this many times. I do envy your good fortune to have loved such a woman.

As I feared, my long-arranged trip to South America will preclude my attendance at Carole's funeral. I understand that you may wish for a private family affair, but I would have been privileged to attend had I been in the country. Perhaps we two shall meet one day in happier circumstances.

I hope the knowledge that Carole was held in such high regard, nay loved, by so many colleagues can comfort you in your grief. She was our compadre, a good companion, a treasure.

Yours most sincerely,

Graeme Robledo-Brown

For our last holiday before our son was born Carole and I scratched enough together to afford a ten-day trip to India. I can say, therefore, without fear of contradiction, that fifty foot scaffolding towers made of bamboo were, and perhaps still are, the norm rather than the exception on building sites in that enchanting country. They are the scariest things: laughing in the face of the horizontal and the vertical, they seem to bend and sway, even in the lightest breeze, like the neck of a charmed cobra as they rise recklessly heavenwards. Bound together with rope (I even saw twine and rags in one village), they defy gravity, wind and rain. Squadrons of lithe acrobats in coolie hats carrying buckets of cement six, eight, ten storeys off the ground spring around the frames as happily as if they were dancing on the brown dirt so far below.

Today I cannot walk past a scaffolding tower without breaking out in a cold sweat. Not since the inane accident which killed my wife. I have read the descriptions from several points of view, listened to the statements from even more, studied all of the photographs taken at the scene. And so I can relive it all, the sounds, the sights, the shock in perfect clarity even though I was over a hundred miles away from the epicentre.

As Carole's escort through the streets of central London on that damp, dismal day, Graeme Robledo was the most reliable witness and it is his account which, to my mind, holds most truth. Although disputed by the site manager, other passers-by corroborated his version of the sickening events. They have formed for me, ever since, a short, shaky mental video-clip which runs intermittently, unexpectedly, on automatic.

It is an oppressive afternoon. Carole and Robledo are saun-tering together towards Oxford Circus, chatting, laughing, hand in hand. (There are two versions of the video; one is less intimate.) The conference is over. They have a little time before she needs to catch her train home. Perhaps time for him to buy them both a cappuccino, or for a giggly moment or two shared in a bookshop. He whispers in her ear: he knows a little Span-ish wine bar in this neighbourhood where they do divine tapas; relaxed ambiance, soft lighting, his treat. Could she perhaps take the later train? She pushes him away playfully and then grabs the sleeve of his jacket and pulls him close again. Now they are approaching an obstacle on the pavement: a set of scaffolding, three floors high and fifteen metres in length rises from the footpath, flanking a high building - the ground floor is a furniture shop - whose second-storey windows are being replaced by a team of two or three hard-hats in scuffed yellow vests. Carole and Robledo are aware of the pavement closure. The lower standards are bandaged in red and white plastic tape, and the pair are guided, as are all pedestrians, by arrowed panels into the road to follow a coned-off strip along the kerb-side. Robledo pauses theatrically, the true gentleman, to allow Carole to step ahead. Which she does, with fatal consequences.

There is a metallic crack, then a sharp shattering of steel and wood, a splinter of a second even before she moves, but it is not enough warning. A workman shouts, a second screams, out of control, a creaking section of loose scaffolding collapses like a matchstick model, and planks, tubing, ladders, tools, debris and finally a flailing, tumbling man hit the road with a clattering, a crashing, a heavy thud. Trapped in the moment, Carole has no time to react. Robledo's instinct is to step back, but he too is hit by a steel pipe and is knocked to the kerb. He groans, he's broken something, a shoulder, a collarbone? But Carole is not so lucky. She is part-buried beneath the sudden shower of metal and wood and dust. Robledo looks up, hears a low moan, but this is from the labourer. He has fallen fourteen feet, his body lies twisted like a tormented rag doll, but his fall has been broken by the contorted silent woman beneath him. He is breathing, whining for help.

As pedestrians converge on the scene, as the other build-ers scamper down a ladder from the portion of scaffolding that remains intact, as Robledo groggily gets to his feet, the video-clip darkens to black. The shouting, the traffic noise, the clink-clang of drill bits and jemmies still raining down, bouncing off the ground - all quickly fade to silence.

I was told that the impact wasn't in itself fatal; although terribly injured, Carole was still breathing when the para-medics arrived. She died from a heart attack in the ambu-lance, with Robledo sobbing at her side.

There was no argument about the cause of death, but sadly the liability was cursorily disputed. It was obvious that the scaffolding had been erected, earlier that very morning as it happened, in haste, that is to say inadequately. It had been raining, so the rain was blamed. The couplers could not be tightened fully with wet tools, the planks were slip-pery. On top of that the work was not checked by a super-visor. The details really don't matter anymore. Nevertheless the site manager insisted that Carole had actually bumped hard into an upright as she stepped off the pavement. It was a ludicrous assertion, and thankfully one that was swept away by the majority view. The legal exchanges were brief, and the company swiftly, mercifully, accepted full responsibility.

Like a damp match, my anger wouldn't ignite. It hasn't really manifested itself even now, more than a year on. Even my grief was stifled. There was a sudden void not only in my life but also in my soul. Who was I to be angry with? A trainee scaffolder for whom time meant money?

Or Robledo for encouraging my wife *off piste*? Or Carole for being in London in the first place? Or God, once again playing the lazy puppeteer with mankind, master of his vaguely arbitrary universe? It was a senseless, absurd, stupid death - a death to exasperate rather than to anger. There were moments when I blamed myself. If I hadn't retired so early she wouldn't have had to compensate. She wouldn't have had to spread herself so thin. Did others think in this way? I sometimes felt that such an idea had crept through Gabriel's mind.

Robledo was a dignified man. An educated man. I spoke to him on the phone on several occasions. He said all the right things to the police, to the solicitors, and to me. But I have never met him and I probably never will. I remember he wrote one unnerving letter to me before Carole's funeral to apologise in advance for his absence. Truthfully, I am glad he was to be abroad on the day. How to deal with him face to face? How far would my respect, my trust have stretched? If I had confronted him with my flimsy suspicions about his relationship with my wife (the funeral would have been the most inappropriate time, in any case), he would have had only to deny them with studied disbelief, with measured disdain, with calculated humour and I would have been left a floundering clod, embarrassed and humiliated less by her infidelity than by his intellect.

Just three months into retirement I found myself entirely alone. That's a little unfair on the small number of friends who rallied round, and on my son and his family too. But nobody could really reach me and help recharge the empty cell that my life had suddenly become. I missed work more than ever. I had moments of bitter regret that I had stopped too soon. I even missed Coppinger. I thought about offering my services part-time, as and when, if ever they were short of manpower, reduced pay not a problem. Then I would remember the reasons why I had quit and realised I'd been right to all along.

Of course I missed Carole too. The house was too large, the kitchen too quiet, the bedroom too neat. The single toothbrush in the mug on the bathroom shelf looked bereft. Until I erased it her voice was still on the answering machine, a remnant of her life force, confident, polished like an actor's, with a hint of her irony: *This is Carole and Don's. We're both of us out at the moment but a little message might just do the trick.* In my loneliness I listened to her voice a few times to fill a silence but it was just too macabre. The end of July brought lovely long sunny days but without her I couldn't face the holiday we had planned. If I ever had been her *big, burly, heroic teddy bear*, here I was with the stuffing ripped right out of me. I had too much time and no deadlines to meet, too much space and no directions to follow, so much pointless freedom that it hurt.

Then the money began to fall into my lap: unearned money, a fatuous windfall. Firstly Carole's life insurance paid up with very little prompting. Secondly the huge compensation payment arrived. Taken together these additions swelled our... *my* bank account by over a quarter of a million pounds. This was only the half of it. A letter from the Teachers' Pensions Agency added to my confusion by mentioning an in-service Death Grant on top of eventual access to a significant pension fund. When I talked of retirement, of stopping earning, we had calculated the risk to the payments of the stubborn tail-end of our mortgage; now, implausibly, I could pay off the balance at a stroke. It was crazy. How ironic that not so very long after I had ceased to contribute to the household budget, I found myself accessing an account holding the largest amount of wealth I had ever owned. Suddenly, dizzyingly, I had more money than I knew what to do with.

ELEVEN

The scene plays in the lounge bar of a quiet country pub. It is even quieter than usual this evening, but it is still early. Above the bar a clock face fashioned from the wooden lid of an ancient beer cask is indicating twenty minutes past seven. One or two couples are eating dinner choices and in a side room a group of lads are playing pool, their muffled voices rising and falling in rhythm with the game. Meanwhile in a corner by the fire, flickering orange in its iron hearth, sit Don Percey and Geena Dale, facing one another across a small circular table, just wide enough for a pair of matching place settings. A book-sized menu stands open between them like the net on a tennis court. There is no food on this table, however, and no prospect of any. Don seems a little fidgety, trying to get comfortable on the cushionless chair, fiddling with a couple of beer mats while he nurses a pint of bitter. Geena is taking a sip of lager. She looks the more relaxed and has an easy smile which widens as an old black Labrador wanders over, gives them both a cursory inspection and, unimpressed, slouches down in front of the fireplace. A little music has already faded out and the click-clack-thud of the pool table provides instead an intermittent background noise. Don is coughing to clear his throat but it is Geena whose voice is heard:

"This is a nice little pub," she says.

"Yeah," he nods, "and not too far for either of us."

"It *is* a bit out of the way, Don."

"What do you mean?" he says, slow to spot that she is teasing him.

"You know, off the beaten track."

"Oh. Not really."

"You ashamed to be seen with me, then?"

"No, not at all," he says behind a hollow laugh. "Not at all. No, I did want to be discreet though."

"Discreet? Why?"

Don ignores the question, shuffles on his seat and takes a drink from his glass.

"I'm glad you agreed to come," he says presently.

"Well it's not every day I get invited out on a date," she rolls on, still making mischief.

"It's not really a date…"

"I'm jokin', Don," she smiles. "It's all a bit mysterious, though, ain't it?"

He sips again, swallows and straightens up on the chair.

"I wanted to talk to you, Geena."

"You could have done that at home. Or on the phone."

"No, I couldn't. Not properly. Definitely not on the phone. You never know where yours is!"

She is glad he has finally made a light-hearted comment. But she is still unsure as to where this talk is heading.

"That's very true! Actually, I do have it somewhere here in my bag tonight."

"Amazing!"

"But I don't have a right lot of credit on it."

"I rest my case."

The dog looks up to see what the woman is scratching around in her handbag for, but she has already given up.

"I wanted to talk to you properly. Quietly."

"Oh. Quietly," she says with an apologetic smile. "I'm not sure if I do *quietly*."

"Of course you do, Geena. But you don't do it often enough."

"Really?" She is off balance. "Have you brought me out here to judge me?"

"No, not at all. Sorry. Look, please don't take this the wrong way..."

"Take what?"

Don hesitates, looks up from his glass, his eyes meet hers, uncertain:

"I'd like to help you."

"I thought this was about Polo," says Geena, looking puzzled.

"Well, it is, in a way..."

"You think we need help, do you?" she asks, suddenly affronted. "You think *I* need help?"

"Well, no, I don't mean you're *helpless*."

"What *do* you mean, *help me*?" She has become as brittle as an icicle. "You mean help me with money, is that it? You think I'm a charity case, Don? Is that it? I'm not, alright?"

"No, no, I'm not saying that..."

"I don't want your pity, or anybody else's."

"No, of course not. Look, this is coming out wrong. I'm sorry. I'm not being *charitable*. I'm just trying to be *kind*. And it's not about pity. I just want to be able to give you a helping hand."

He is trying to look hard into her eyes, but he is wobbling and she is still defensive.

"A helpin' hand?"

"Listen, Geena. Please just stop and listen to me. This is hard, and the last thing I want to do is patronise you and your family…"

"My family? My whole family now?"

Don takes a deep breath, folds up the menu and places it flat on the table, out of the way.

"Listen," he says, "I've got to know you a bit in the last few months and I like you. I like you and the children. I think you've had a rough time and you deserve better. I want to help you get on your feet."

"You think we're on our knees?"

"No. Don't be obtuse."

"Ob-what?"

"Don't put up barriers. You know what I mean. Your life could be, should be so much better. You deserve more. You deserve a new washing machine, for a start."

Geena laughs, and Don's smile is one of relief.

"That's true. Bloody thing rattles like a box of nails."

They both pause for a drink.

"And something nice for your little granddaughter," suggests Don.

"Oh, don't go on about Lily! Granddaughter! It makes me sound like I'm ancient!"

"And a holiday," he adds, seizing the moment. "Polo needs a proper holiday, don't you think? He's a bright boy, he needs some stimulation, some excitement, a chance to see more than just his village…"

Now Geena is straightening up in her seat, registering his drift:

"You're sayin' I'm a shit mother."

"No, no, I'm not! Not at all! I'm saying you've had a rough deal and you deserve more because you're a nice person, a good person deep down. I know you are."

"You know? You *know* I'm a nice person? Well, I'm flattered, Don, but I'm not sure it's true."

"What do you mean?"

Now Geena pauses to take a long breath.

"Don, you're a kind man," she says quietly. "But really, you don't want to get mixed up with me. Trust me, I'm trouble. You *don't* know me. You're closer to it when you call me a shit mother..."

"I didn't say that. You know I didn't..."

"Listen, I've got kids I can't control, I owe a fortune, I've got a shitty job, I've got a police record from way back, I did drugs, I can't stop smokin' – I've tried, believe me – some of my friends are lowlifes, I admit, I can't keep a man, I break stuff..."

She tails away, then repeats:

"I break stuff, yeah? That's what I do, Don. All the time. I break stuff."

"Don't. That's not the woman I see. I see a woman who's been dealt a poor hand and who is struggling to make the best of it."

She is staring down at her glass, held tightly in both hands. Don has more:

"Look, you've kicked the drugs, you've got a job, you've got a son, Kenny, isn't it? – who is a credit to you, and Polo and

119

Amber will turn out great, I know it. And they love you to bits. Don't they?"

Geena smiles weakly through her self-contempt.

"Yeah. Yeah, they do."

"And even Angelo, on his good days," he says, reflecting her smile.

"Let's not get carried away…"

Don notices that she has started to cry.

"Hey, don't. I don't want to upset you, Geena. That's the last thing I want…"

"I'm not upset. I just get like this, I can't help myself. I can't stop myself from blubbin' if someone says somethin' nice about my kids."

"More than if they say something nasty?"

"I'm used to that. I'm not so used to compliments."

She laughs, picks up a table napkin and wipes her eyes and nose.

"They're good kids," Don goes on. "And you, you've got a lovely spunky attitude, a fighting spirit, you're kind and you're warm-hearted. Don't knock yourself, Geena. Don't do yourself down."

She is becoming self-conscious. She blows her nose and takes a deep breath as if to absorb this amount of flattery.

"'Scuse me a sec," she says, standing. "I need the loo. Just give me a minute."

"Of course. Shall I get you another drink?"

"No. No, thanks. Better not."

*

The same scene. One of the pool players is standing at the bar buying a round of drinks. The dog has fallen asleep and is gently snoring. Geena has returned. She has made a poor job of wiping away her smudged mascara. She has removed the little scarf she had been wearing and has loosened a couple of buttons on her blouse. Ever the detective, Don has noticed all these fine details.

"So then, Mr Don Percey," she says, regaining her composure, "you want to buy me a new washin' machine, do you?"

"Well, it would be a start," he replies, smiling. "Wouldn't it?"

"Would it?"

"Yes, it would."

"An' where would it end?"

Don, who has no idea, avoids the question and presses on:

"I'd like to pay the bill for the broken windows at school too."

"Oh, I've paid that already. Weeks ago."

"Yes, but probably at the expense of something else you'd have wanted to spend it on, eh? At Christmas?"

Geena looks down at her half-empty glass.

"And your car looks like it needs some money spending on it."

"Don," she says, looking up at him again. "I'm not askin' for this, you know? You don't need to do this. Any of it. We'll manage. Spend your money on yourself, yeah? On your own family. On your own grandson."

"Geena, listen. I've got plenty of money. Since my wife died I've become quite a wealthy man. I know it might sound daft but I've got far more money than I need. And I want to do something positive with it. Something positive for you. For your family. Something life-changing."

She is suddenly very nervous about such a big word.

"Life-changin'?"

"Yeah. I don't want just to give you handouts for washing machines and garage bills. I want to make a proper difference."

"Sounds serious."

"I am being."

"An' what do you want from me in return?"

"Nothing."

"Nothin'?"

"Nothing."

"You sure?"

"Nothing. I mean it."

Geena pauses, then lowers her voice to ask:

"Since your wife died, Don, have you become a *very* lonely man?"

"I want nothing from you, Geena. Absolutely no strings attached."

"You for real? That don't sound like a *man* talkin'."

"No strings. Except that you take the chance I'm giving you to do right by Polo and Amber. And yourself."

"Do right?"

"Yeah, move on from the way things have been. I'm giving you the chance to move away from The Pavilions, to get somewhere nicer, put down a deposit…"

"Hang on, Don. I like it where we live."

"Do you? Really?"

"Anyway, how can I afford to move? I can't even afford a new doormat."

"Listen, Geena. This is my proposition. I've got enough money, so don't worry about that. All the money you'll need. And there are no strings. Honestly." He looks her firmly in the eyes, and speaks the words he has been rehearsing for weeks:

"I'd like to give you £10,000…"

"Ten thousand?" she mouths the number in alarm.

"Yes, £10,000 *per year*. For the next ten years. The children will be grown up by then, you'll be comfortable, they can have a good life…"

There is a moment. There has to be a moment. Just a brief moment when the chink of cutlery falls silent, the flames in the hearth burn cold, there is no click-clack-thump from the pool room, the dog stops snoring, the hands on the beer cask clock face freeze. Only the heart inside Don's chest keeps pounding, and Geena's too, of course, fitfully, unbridled. Now the moment is already passed and exasperation is the new tone in her voice:

"£10,000, for ten years? Don, don't be ridiculous! I couldn't possibly take it. You're out of your mind!"

"I'm not being ridiculous," he insists, unmoved.

"Yes, you are." There is anger now in her words. "Fuck, you are. It's crazy money. It's scary. It's mad. I could never begin to pay it back…"

"Haven't you been listening? I don't *want* you to pay it back! Not a penny."

But Geena has already stopped listening to him. She stands, grabs her bag and makes to leave.

"You're mad. It's too weird. I told you I'm not a charity case,

Don, but you don't get it. You're scarin' me. I'm goin' home."

"But…"

"You stay here. You finish your drink, yeah? I don't want your money. I don't. I like the way I am, you understand that? Shit, I need a cigarette."

And before Don can speak again, she has walked away, across the room, out through the door and into the car park.

*

Less than a minute later, Don is out in the car park which is faintly lit by a single carriage light on the wall of the building. A faint tang of wood-smoke drifts in the air. In the shadows Geena is standing by her car, the people carrier, key already in the lock. Don is running towards her anxiously, calling before he has caught his breath:

"Geena, don't go like this! Please. I'm sorry if I scared you. Look, forget it. Forget the whole conversation. Forget we ever came here. I made a mistake, I can see that. I'm really sorry. Please."

The woman opens the car door and her face is lit by the interior light. She is breathing normally, she can sense that he is already by her side, she turns to him.

"Okay. I'll forget it. And you must as well. Let me live my life my way."

"Okay. And I'm sorry."

"You don't need to say sorry, Don."

"Okay."

"Look, don't think I'm not grateful. It's very sweet, too sweet, but I can't take your money. You get it, don't you? I don't want to owe people."

"But I said…"

"Owe them, not just owe money. Owe *them*." She offers him a brief smile. "I want to keep my pride, Don. My own worth, yeah? Whatever you or anyone else might think that means. I don't want to lose that."

Don takes a step back.

"I understand. I'm sorry, but I do understand."

"Good."

"And let's not talk about this to anybody else. Don't mention it to Polo."

"Of course I won't."

"Or anybody else."

"Anybody else?"

"A friend…, a boyfriend…"

"A boyfriend? You mean Sharky?"

It's the first time he has heard her say his name.

"Whoever. Whoever you're seeing."

Geena laughs, as sincerely as she has since she arrived here.

"Sharky! He'd go mad if I told him you were makin' *propositions*!"

"I said there were no strings."

"Don, I'm jokin'! Let's leave it, yeah? You're a lovely man but I think you need to get your head straight. An' so do I. Come here."

She opens her arms to him and they hug loosely.

"Oh, there's these," says Don, handing her a paper bag. "I bought a couple of little books for Amber. You said she was a reader. Carole bought the same ones for Oliver, so I know they'll be good."

"Don, what are you like?"

"So you'll take these at least?"

"Yeah, of course," she says, offering him an indulgent smile. "Amber'll be thrilled to bits."

"I hope so."

"She will."

"Well, thank you."

"Thank *you*, you mean. It's very sweet."

She takes the gift, turns and settles into her car.

"I'll see you tomorrow."

Don watches her clip herself in and switch on the headlights.

"Yeah, I suppose you will. Can you promise me one other thing? Can you promise to stop smoking around her? You know, for her asthma? It's doing her no good…"

"Don, leave it. She's not your kid. She's my kid, yeah? Look, thanks for the drink. I'll see you in the mornin'."

She pulls the door shut, revs the engine hard, drives out on to the lane and accelerates away into the night. Don stands in the cold air watching her tail-lights disappear, listening to the harsh rattle of the engine that shreds the silence long after the image has faded.

COUNTY HOSPITAL

Only once have I stepped over the threshold of Geena Dale's home in The Pavilions. It was early April, the first week back after the Easter holidays. A Friday, I think; the Friday of Polo's class trip to Corfe Castle, the trip he had been talking to us about all week long, explaining which side it had been on in the English Civil War (the Cavaliers) and what had happened to it after the siege (it was demolished). When the day came the forecast was for rain, and at the last minute Geena ran out to the minibus and stuffed a kagoul into Polo's schoolbag. I remember him groaning. *Don't lose it, it's your brother's*, she said with a mad wave.

Polo didn't lose it, probably didn't wear it, even when the showers arrived at lunchtime. What he did do, though, by accident I am sure, was leave it on my bus. He'd been in a sulk about something and had sat at the back wanting to talk to nobody. The coat was screwed up and wedged down the side of his seat almost out of sight and I only noticed it when I was back at the yard tidying up for the end of the week. Rita hadn't noticed it either; mind you, she was always in a hurry to get off on a Friday afternoon. The coat could wait till Monday, but I thought of the boy getting not only an earful from his mother but having Angelo on his case as well. I was in no particular rush to go home to my meal for one in a big empty house so I decided to get into my car and retrace my route to his village.

Down at the houses I could hear the sound of what I thought was American rap music before I had got out of my car. It seemed to be coming from No.5. Outside No.3 the neighbour with the face piercings was leaning against the wall, talking to a teenage boy with a cigarette in her mouth. As I rapped on Geena's door she looked towards me with a snarl on her lips, or maybe it was a sly smile framing her chipped tooth. The youth was already sloping off down the lane, hands tucked deep into the pockets of his sloppy tracksuit bottoms. Her expression to me wordlessly yet eloquently posed the question: *What you doin' down here off limits, out of hours, then?* And with the slight raising of a pierced eyebrow, the protective follow-up: *You botherin' Geena?* Instead of speaking to me she called after the boy, something cheeky, probably obscene, and then tossed her cigarette end out on to the damp grass. Fortunately some-one answered the door before I felt obliged to engage with her.

It was Amber, still in her school uniform, looking up at me from waist height.

"Hello," she said.

"Hello, Amber. Is your mum in?" I asked.

"How you know my name?"

"I just do," I smiled.

Geena was taken aback to see me. I explained about the raincoat (*Oh, you shouldn't have bothered. It could've waited till Monday*) and we could have left it at that, but she invited me in so that I could hand it to Polo personally. The house was even smaller inside than it looked from the path. I had been in houses like this many times before: the walls were thin and blank, the floors bare but for one or two cheap mats and discarded clothes, and the heating was on high, which seemed to exaggerate the smell of cooking oil and domestic animals. On cue a scruffy ginger cat ran up the stairs. Instinctively Geena laughed and apologised for the mess. She had come from the kitchen where she'd been making the kids' tea: chicken nuggets, bread and butter. She seemed nervous, distracted, pulling at her earlobe as she spoke to me. I found Polo in the living room. Damp had stained a patch of grey under the window ledge and on the far wall there was a single decoration: a large black and white print of the famous photo of Marilyn Monroe standing over a subway vent in New York City with her skirt billowing up.

The boy was lying on a boxy leatherette sofa watching cartoons on TV. It was their new set, I was guessing, a flat-screen monster with a brand name I had never heard of, possibly North Korean. There was a vertical crack on the screen from top to bottom and an inch or two of misting along the line of the break. Geena saw me looking at it. *It's goin' back next week*, she said. *Bloody rubbish. I reckon they bashed it when they carried it in. We've only had it five minutes.* Polo took the kagoul off me. *Say thank you, Polo*, she said. I smiled. I think he was just about to anyway. He seemed shy, disoriented to see his school bus driver standing in his mother's living room. There was no sign of Angelo, and Amber complained she was thirsty and disappeared into the kitchen.

I stayed for no more than a minute. As I left we wished each other a nice weekend. Quite by surprise Geena took my hand at the front door. I noticed hers was a little sticky from the cooking. *Thank you, Don*, she smiled. *You didn't need to come. But the fact you did tells me you're a proper nice fella.*

The meeting I had with Geena Dale in The Royal Oak a week or two later was a disaster. I can remember it vividly. I had chosen the pub because it was on the forest road a good ten miles from her village and I didn't want us to be recognised. Was I embarrassed to be seen with her? I don't know, but I was confused. I wasn't even sure that she'd turn up. It was a Monday, mercifully a quiet night for drinkers, and I'd had the chance to ask her that very morning. Rita was settling the children down and Geena came round to the driver's window to pass the time of day. I couldn't just ask her there and then - and here's the element of premeditation - so I passed her a note I'd written and told her to go inside and read it.

Dear Geena,

Please don't think I am interfering but I would like to talk to you properly about Polo. As you know, we seem to get along pretty well on the bus, the pair of us, and I am concerned about him. I can't talk at your house obviously, and was hoping that you would be free to meet me for a quiet drink tonight.

I suggest The Royal Oak on the lower forest road. I will be there at 7 o'clock.

If you cannot come, please ring this number (---) and we can find another time. Sorry for the short notice, but it is important.

Sincerely,

Don Percey

I remember it word for word. I rewrote it three or four times. Whatever I did, I didn't want to frame it as an invitation for a date. I wanted a neutral tone. And I felt bad, even with the final draft, for using Polo as the bait.

So how did it come to this?

The money was burning a hole in my pocket. I had never owned so much. And I quickly arrived at the conclusion that I didn't need most of it. The house was paid for now, mortgage-free, and anyway without Carole to share it was too big. Downsizing wouldn't cost me anything; quite the reverse. I had plenty to spend on myself, travel plans (vague and sparse) and luxuries (minimal). I was never one for luxuries. I preferred to buy stuff that lasted. Gabe and Grace were comfortable enough, I calculated: he's got a steady job, she's got rich parents, they're fine. They'd inherit a decent sum anyway, and there's money for little Oliver. Just how much money do people actually need to live?

What drives a man to want more than enough, and then still want more? Competitiveness? Greed? I often found myself mulling over a dichotomy of modern society (I had plenty of time on my hands): the rights of wrongs of the heads and tails of capitalism and socialism.

There must be a very good case in a civilised society for the necessities of life to be provided by the community as a whole for each individual member of that community, that is, by the state: education, health care and security, for example. And then, why not the supply of water and electricity, why not transport and housing and communications, with profits reinvested into improvements and development? Are state monopolies a bad thing?

The capitalist will point to the need for consumer choice, the driver that is competition, how the profit motive breeds innovation and fosters individual brilliance. He will talk of corruption, inefficiency and stagnation in sectors that run blindly along on state aid. The socialist in turn will highlight capitalism's exploitation of labour, the creation of extremes of wealth and poverty, the desolation of the system's losers, and, in times of crisis, the irony of the state stepping in to rescue private companies deemed too important to fail, for example large banks, in what someone clever described as *corporate socialism* or *socialism for the rich.* In the same breath was mentioned the use of tax credits and housing benefit as state-funded subsidies to exploitative employers and landlords.

It seems to me that we are still a long way from a sensible compromise. Two hundred years of industrialisation have not been nearly enough for us to evolve beyond destructive tribal conflicts. The human condition is still one where animal instincts battle with something nobler, more reasoned. Even the wisest, the saintliest, the most well-balanced, the most selfless modern man is little more than an earnest, endless adolescent staggering drunk on his own

131

self-importance from one fuck-up to the next.

In the end you can only do what you can do: my profound conclusion!

I considered donating a large amount to charity. But which one? I had no affinity to any one special interest group and I felt I needed to do something personal not institutional. On reflection, I know I was closing doors without really looking behind them to see what was there. And I gave little thought to the future. How bad could a rainy day be?

So this half-hearted dithering, this vapid process of going through the motions, was doomed from the outset; my mind, unclear at first and swirling like a winter fog, was already made up, gradually crystallizing harder each passing day that I drove to pick up that boy at No.1 The Pavilions. It was more than a whim. It felt right. It was a noble cause. And she was worth it. She deserved something better than a life strangled between the thin walls of that scruffy box. I could open the trap for her, and I wanted to. But I needed to be sensitive.

Geena arrived on time. The pub was not busy and we found a corner table. She had made an effort to look her best, I noticed. I had rarely seen her wearing lipstick, and her hair, still fair, was tied back and bunched in a glitzy elasticated band. The red marks on her wrists had disappeared. She wore a skirt that she sometimes went to work in, but I had not seen her blouse before: a pink floral, tight and buttoned almost to the collar. And at her pretty neck a thin navy scarf, tied as a choker. She later told me she had borrowed both items from Angelo's girlfriend.

How do you offer somebody £100,000 without embarrassing them? Well, I failed, so I can't say. Of course I didn't offer her so much to start with, but just letting her know that I wanted to contribute even a little to her family without humiliating her was an ordeal. At this stage I believe she was onside, but there was still confusion over any quid pro quo. I did insist I wanted nothing in return, but it was no coincidence that when she returned from the ladies the neck scarf had vanished and she had unbuttoned her blouse to display more than a shadow of cleavage.

Unnerved but determined, I ploughed on, only to spook her with the huge offer. I was genuine, of course, but I can see that it was too much to digest. Instead, Geena took fright and fled. I don't believe Sharky had anything to do with it. In fact I regretted even mentioning him, but I was desperate for our meeting to remain private. I'd never seen him at that stage, although Polo had mentioned his name in the days before. I had noticed a scrambling bike parked under the kitchen window on more than one occasion and asked the boy, nonchalantly, who it belonged to. It was Sharky's. Sharky? *Yeah, my mum's boyfriend. He stays some nights. It's a cool bike, innit? Kawasaki. Japanese.* I did see him days later, of course, lolling on the mud-splattered machine in heavy sunglasses, cigarette hand dangling dangerously close to the fuel tank. As for the ill-fated rendezvous, I realized that I'd been the one playing with fire.

In the end it was me who felt embarrassed and humiliated, but to her credit when she saw me the following morning, padding out to the bus in her dressing gown and slippers, Geena Dale smiled, said *hi* to me and behaved as though nothing untoward had ever happened.

TWELVE

The scene plays in the comfortable lounge of Gabe's home. Both Don and his son have been drinking percolated coffee, one of the special Javan Arabica blends the younger Percey will often pick up in bulk whenever he has meetings in London. Don would say he's wasting his money but he tends to keep his opinions to himself: *why bother when you get the same taste from an instant at a fraction of the price?* It must be a Saturday morning, they must have been discussing the afternoon's sport, among other things. From the open kitchen door the reassuring, sweet smell of baking drifts into the room. Just as the last drop of coffee passes his lips, just as the conversation reaches a natural lull, Don's grandson Oliver skips through the doorway and it is his excitable, high-pitched voice which comes into focus.

"Grandad," he starts, "do you want the good news first or the bad news?"

Don smiles, and raises an eyebrow to Gabe.

"Where's he got that turn of phrase from?"

"Dunno," says Gabe, chuckling. "Probably TV. Or school. He does pick things up fast."

"Grandad," repeats the little boy, already becoming impatient. "I said do you want to know the good news first or the bad news?"

"Let's have the good news first, shall we?"

"I can swim a width! I did it!"

"You can swim a width! That's brilliant, Ollie!"

"Yes I did," he rattles on, breathlessly. "I swimmed a width at the pool last week. I did it. Without stopping!"

"With armbands?"

"Don't be silly, Grandad." Don has asked a stupid question and the boy couldn't be more offended. "I don't need armbands anymore. Armbands are for babies."

"Well, that's great, young man."

"And Sonia says I can swim a length soon."

"Sonia?"

"She's their teacher," says Gabe. "At the swim club."

"Sonia's my *coach*," insists the boy, making Don laugh.

"Oh, she's your *coach*, is she?"

"She's a champion. Everyone says. Sonia says I can try a length soon. Did she say next week, Daddy?"

"Did she? I don't remember. Yeah, he's a good little swimmer," he says to Don, and then addressing Oliver again, "Aren't you, mate?"

The boy nods.

"So, Ollie," Don resumes, "that's the good news. So what's the bad news?"

But the child has more to add, without breaking his stride:

"Next week or the week after."

"What's that?"

"Trying a length, Grandad."

"Oh."

"Mummy said she'd buy me some new trunks."

"Oh, did she?"

"Olympic ones."

"Very smart."

Oliver has suddenly run out of words, and Gabe and Don exchange a smile.

"And what's the bad news, Oliver?"

"Erm…"

"Perhaps there *is* no bad news?"

"Erm… I forgot."

The boy looks confused, screwing up his face in concentration; he is puzzled that his memory has failed him.

"You only get half the story with Ollie!" notes his father.

"It doesn't matter. Tell me later. Tell me when you remember, eh?"

"Ollie, why don't you go and see if Mummy needs some help in the kitchen? She's baking scones, isn't she? Go and see what she's up to."

Oliver scampers off into the kitchen as Gabe tidies up the weekend's papers, which are scattered around the room. Stacking them on a coffee table, he sits in an armchair close to his father.

"So, Dad," he resumes, "you said you had something you wanted to tell me?"

"Well, you *and* Grace."

Grace appears on cue, wiping her hands with a tea towel. Her Saturday morning look involves no make-up, her hair is tied up in a loose knot, her shirt sleeves are still rolled up to the elbow; she looks tired.

"Here I am. Cakes in the oven."

"Where's Ollie?" asks her husband.

"He went straight outside. He's on the swing. He's fine."

She plumps up a pair of cushions then settles down on the sofa next to her father-in-law, who is clearing his throat.

"Well," he begins," I wanted to let you know that I've made a big decision." Gabe and Grace are glancing at each other. "A big decision about money. About your mum's money. Well, *my* money now."

"What do you mean, Dad?" asks Gabe, intrigued.

"Well, as you know, I have quite suddenly become a wealthy man, and frankly it's money I can do without."

"Do without?"

"Well, money that I want to give away."

"Give away?" echoes Grace, suddenly alert. "What, to a charity or something?"

"Well, not exactly." Don offers a supportive smile to each. "Don't worry, you two. I'll hold some back for you and Oliver. Of course I will. You'll inherit the house for starters when I'm gone..."

"Dad, don't talk like that! You're in your fifties, for God's sake!"

"Well, you'll have to face it one day, son. It might not be the same house, mind you."

"You thinking of moving, Don?" asks Grace.

"Well, no, not immediately. But into something smaller, perhaps. Eventually. We'll see. It's too big for me now, where I am, you can both see that. It was even too big for the three of us when you were still living at home, Gabe."

The younger man needs a moment to take this in.

"Slow down. What are you saying? You'll stay round here, won't you?"

"Of course. No, I'm not planning to leave. Anyway, that's probably years off. Besides, that's not what I'm come over to tell you."

Don shuffles to the edge of his seat, elbows on his knees, and rests his chin in cupped hands. He is addressing his son:

"While I've been driving these past months, you know, the minibus, I've got to meet a lot of new, interesting people…"

"You've mentioned some of them," says Grace. "Funny people, they sound…"

"The little lad Polo you've taken a shine to…" adds Gabe.

"Yes, he's one of them. And there's his mother."

"His mother?"

"And his little sister."

"What about them?" asks Grace.

"Well, she's struggling. You know, to stay afloat. Geena's her name."

Grace again: "Isn't she the woman you said couldn't even get out of bed most mornings?"

"I didn't say that, Grace. She's had a rough life: very little education, poor background, had kids too young, crummy job, dead-end boyfriends, you both know the sort…"

The woman looks towards her husband. They both wait for more, already worried about where Don is heading.

"I think she's great," he is saying. "In spite of all the shitty cards her life has dealt her, she's still fighting against the tide, still doing what she can for her family. She knows there's a better life out there somewhere. I admire her. I admire her spirit, her optimism. She still messes up now and again. Actually all the time. And so does Polo, but they're great. Polo could be a real star. He's a bright lad but he's got such low expectations. He needs stimulation… what he needs is a sense of his own worth."

Gabe hears the affection in his father's voice but is no less anxious:

"And… so…?"

"And so I'm going to give them a leg-up."

"A hand-out?" asks Grace. "What is she, some kind of charity case?"

"She's not a charity case." Don is steadfast. "She's a warm human being who's had quite an impact on me. She needs support and I am in a position to give it to her."

"What's going on, here, Don? Have you fallen for her? You're not saying you're in love with her or anything stupid, are you? Isn't she, well, a bit of a scrubber?"

"Grace!" shouts Gabe. "That's enough!"

Don pauses. He has expected antipathy but is determined to stay calm.

"No, I don't love her, Grace," he says after a moment. "I'm not in love with her. I *like* her. I like her a lot. Okay? Can you understand that? She's not going to take the place of Carole, if that's what you're thinking. And she's not a scrubber. Have some respect."

Gabe is wanting to move on:

"What sort of support, Dad? You're talking about lending her some money?"

"No, not lending her money. Giving it. A donation."

"What do you mean, unconditionally?"

"Well, not unconditionally. It's for her family, their well-being, the kids' education, their development…"

"How much?" asks Grace, her tone edged with aggression.

"How much are you planning to give this woman?"

"I've already offered her a sum. A large sum. But she refused it…"

"She refused it?" says Gabe. "There's gratitude! So let her refuse it! End of story."

"No, it's not the end. She needs money now. Today. For immediate needs like paying bills. She'll change her mind. She'll come round."

"So, how much, Don?" Grace insists. "How much are you giving her *conditionally*?"

"I offered her £10,000."

"Jesus!"

"That's very generous, isn't it, Dad? *Over*-generous?"

"For the next ten years," Don continues, unfazed. "Till Polo's twenty-one."

"What? What do you mean, a grand a year?"

"No, you don't understand. My fault. £10,000 *per year*. So that's £100,000 all in."

"Fuck!" whispers Grace, loudly enough to be heard.

Gabe has his hands to his mouth. The face is turning from pink to white.

"Dad, are you crazy? What were you thinking?"

"I was thinking that this is what I want to do!" he replies, matching fire with fire. "Alright? I was thinking this woman, this family, they're worth it. £10,000 a year for ten years, it could be life-changing. It will be. *That's* what I was thinking."

"It's a fortune, Dad."

"It's *our* fortune," adds Grace bitterly, then, wondering if she has overstepped the mark, "Isn't it, Gabe?"

"I already said you'd be okay," Don runs on. "I can afford it. I've got plenty. I've got too much."

Gabe has to stand. He is scratching the hair at his temples, he is walking to the bay window, he is looking into the avenue but is seeing nothing, he is taking a deep, deep breath.

"Are you absolutely sure you've thought this through?" he says, turning back to face his father. "A hundred grand? I can't believe I'm saying this. One hundred thousand pounds? You could spend it on so many other things. Treat yourself, Dad. Buy a nice car. A camper van or something. Go travelling, go on a cruise... You'd meet people, make new friends..."

"Travelling? Not on my own, thank you."

"Take a friend. Take a group of friends. Treat them all."

Don does not answer. He is pleased that he has remained composed. Grace breaks into the short silence:

"Why don't you give it to a proper charity if you want to give so much away? Save The Children, Barnardo's, if it's the children you're worried about. Or the one with the bear with the eye-patch..."

"Children In Need," suggests Gabe in support.

"I'm worried about *these* children. Not faceless children I've never met."

"Or a charity for battered wives," adds Gabe.

"She's not a battered wife, for God's sake!"

"Dad, calm down. I'm sorry."

"And what about Oliver's education?" Grace tosses in, altering the angle and irritating her husband.

"Grace, we don't need to bring Dad into that."

"Well, yes, I think we do. It's exactly what we need to do."

"What do you mean?" Now Don is asking questions.

"We thought…"

"*You* thought."

"*We* thought," she pushes on, "that when Oliver is thirteen you might want to contribute to *his* education."

"Thirteen?" wonders Don. "He'll be at Green Bank by then."

Grace laughs dismissively.

"Green Bank? Are you joking, Don? It's an absolute pit of a school. Oliver is *not* going to Green Bank."

"Sorry, Dad," says Gabe. "This is an ongoing discussion. Between Grace and me."

In spite of her husband's glare towards her, Grace has more:

"Mummy has promised to pay for Oliver's prep school fees, Don, once he's nine."
"Prep school?"

"So that'll take him to thirteen," she drives on.

"It's not decided," says Gabe quietly.

"And we thought – don't deny this, Gabe – we thought that some of your money from Carole's accident – God rest her soul – some of that money could cover him at senior."

"Did you?"

"Our son will not be going to Green Bank. There's no argument. Carole would have understood."

"Leave it, Grace," says Gabe. "Just leave it. We'll talk about this some other time. The boy is six, for Christ's sake."

"Seven in June," she reminds them both.

"Well," says Don, "From what I know about boarding school fees a hundred thousand won't get even him part way into the sixth form."

"It would help. Anyway, he wouldn't necessarily board full-time."

"I can see you've been giving all of this quite a lot of thought, Grace."

"No harm in that. It's your only grandchild's future we're talking about."

Gabe has nothing to say on the subject. He has already wandered back over to the window, through which he is staring angrily into space.

"Grace, I think I'll bail out of this conversation, if you don't mind," concludes Don. He stands and walks over to his son. "I've said what I wanted you say. I didn't expect you to be overjoyed, Gabe, but I thought you might understand. It is my money and I will decide how I spend it."

"It's Carole's money," says Grace, relentlessly. "I can't imagine what she would think."

"Grace, you've said enough," states Don. "I'm sorry you feel this way, but if my mind was ever wavering a bit, well, it's made up now."

Gabe turns away from the window to face his wife, who has started to tremble, and his father, whose self-control has surprised him.

"You said you haven't given her a penny yet, this Tina?"

"*Geena.* Her name is Geena. No, not yet. But I will do. Look, I've upset you. I'm sorry. Just imagine the money was never there. This time last year it wasn't."

"But Mum was…"

And suddenly there are a hundred places Don would rather be. He picks up his jacket from the arm of the sofa and makes to leave:

"Yes. Yes, she was. You're right. And the money wasn't.

Whatever you never had you don't miss. I'm sorry I've spoilt your weekend. I didn't have to tell you anything, and perhaps I shouldn't have bothered. But at least now you know."

"I appreciate it, Dad," sighs Gabe, trying to mend fences, "but I still don't get it."

"You will, I hope. Or maybe you won't. Whatever. It's my decision, Gabe. I've made it."

On any other occasion he would take his leave with a handshake and even a hug, but not today.

"Say goodbye to Ollie for me, won't you?"

COUNTY HOSPITAL

I always remember one of my son Gabriel's schoolmasters at the Grammar commenting in an end-of-term report that he was *a worthy boy, though lacking in flair*. I was mildly upset at the time, but over the years I have conceded that the chap had read him exactly right. It's an epithet that has followed him throughout his thirty years.

Gabe studied geography at university and, once he had sweated blood to secure his degree, he returned directly to the county for a job in local government on the bottom rung of the planning department. After a couple of years and seeing only dead ends ahead of him, he applied for and succeeding in getting a kind of sideways transfer into hospital administration. He works here in this very building where I sit now, still dosed with painkillers. Now that the county hospital NHS trust is having to rationalise its staffing, he is beginning to worry about redundancy. He'll be fine. He's been here six years and is well regarded.

It was at university that he met Grace. Privately educated in one or other of the Home Counties, she was a student of marketing. When they settled in the area her father provided her with the funds to realise her dream of running a small business. In her case it was a shop, a *boutique*, as she preferred to call it, selling high-end children's clothes. She found premises in a renovated arcade, spent a fortune on decor and fittings, and was in her element. Business started slowly, however, and then gradually became even slower. Grace got bored, narrowed her stock, employed a manageress, took a back seat and watched from a safe distance as the losses mounted up. Within eighteen months she sold up, taking, as Gabe quietly admitted to me, *a huge hit*. By this time Oliver had arrived. The shop was rarely mentioned again. She had a new project. Since then, as far as I can see, it's been kindergarten, coffee mornings, toddlers' group, the school run, yoga and retail therapy. Not much else. No work on the horizon. Gabe said she'd nagged for a nanny for Oliver, but it was out of the question.

It took me a long while to stir myself after Carole's accident. I met old friends and tried, with mixed success, to revive what time had already faded. I cleaned up my old bike and went for long rides, sometimes alone and sometimes with a chap in the village who was in training for a triathlon somewhere exotic. Usually alone, to be honest; he was too energetic to keep up with comfortably.

I was vaguely thinking about doing some volunteering at the hospital, driving jobs, part-time, when I spotted Pattermore's advert in the free paper. I spoke to John, fancied it and stepped into the unknown. Not much of a risk, really: I only needed to give a month's notice if I wanted to stop. Gabe was surprised, baffled even. I reminded him that I was still only fifty-four and I wanted to do it for my sanity. I was to start in the September, only three months after Carole's death, and in deference to her - and, I hope, to me - he stifled any reservations and wished me well.

I took up swimming a little more seriously, inspired, I think, by Paul Tufts or perhaps even my grandson Oliver. I cycled to the leisure centre once or twice a week and inelegantly swam up and down the intermediate lane for half an hour or so, or until I got fed up and lost count of the number of lengths I had done. I read a lot: thrillers, crime stories, mainly. I spent hours in the garden, planting vegetables, pruning bushes, digging weeds, but in truth this had always been Carole's domain and I felt like I was somehow trespassing on her patch.

Sometimes there was activity in the garden next door.

If it was Alec Otterbridge fine-tuning his latest off-roader I would usually keep a low profile and become more intensely involved in deadheading as if it were a matter of urgency. With Gaynor I was more sociable but always unnerved if she ever appeared wearing just a skimpy top, the leather wristband and a smudge of sun cream. On a couple of occasions the postman called when she was out, or more likely upstairs on set in the role of Isabella, and he would have to knock and get me to sign for a parcel or two, always from a company called *Pozzitiv Leisure*. If our paths crossed in the gardens she might thank me for helping out in that way; the contents were never divulged, of course. One day she mentioned that Alec was thinking of moving into the solar energy sector; I said something about hoping for a bright future which sadly passed right over her head. The pair of them never seemed to be out in the back together, they never struck me as companionable. Just recently she mentioned that she was looking forward to a week away in the summer: a holiday on the Costa Blanca with a friend. No, Alec wouldn't be going; he reckoned he had too much work on.

Meanwhile I dug out Gabe's old guitar and joined an evening class: Strumming for Beginners. That was good fun. If I ever get out of this place I must rejoin the group; I don't want to get left behind when they start on Clapton's back catalogue.

Finally, I did something that was quite out of character: after a lifetime of being animal-neutral, I bought a cat. I needed some energy in the house, the movement of another life force other than me. At Christmas a neighbour was offering kittens for sale, and I picked out what I thought to be the prettiest: a fluffy black female with bright eyes, a white nose and all four paws of pure white fur. She looked as if she had stepped into tiny ballet shoes. I invented the name Rina, from ballerina, rhyming with Tina and, I've only just noticed, with Geena. I believe that Jill, the lady up the hill, has taken her in since I've been here. That's a lot of cat food I owe her.

In the course of the past year I saw more of Gabe and Grace than I ever used to. They live only half an hour's drive away but we always kept a discreet distance. Now I suppose we need each other a little more. And Ollie adores Rina.

When I told them about my decision to give the money to Geena Dale it was already a fait accompli, but I felt that they had a right to know what I was thinking. That she had told me to keep my money was neither here nor there. I have to say their reaction saddened me; Grace was particularly snotty. She already had one eye on her own inheritance, it seemed. Whether or not she knew how much of a cushion Carole's death had provided - and there's no way she could have known, at least not from me - she had already ear-marked a large proportion of it.

Gabe too was suspicious. He could see no sense in my motives. He rang later that evening to offer a whole range of alternatives: hospital charities, foreign aid charities, charities I had never heard of, even police charities, for God's sake! Grace reckoned I should buy stocks and shares. And finally, because he knew me so well, Gabe mentioned a cause that I had actually considered myself. The village cricket club had started an appeal for donations for a new pavilion. I could buy them one outright. I dismissed it quite rapidly; it was far too grand a gesture from such a mediocre player whose involvement had dwindled to that of irregular spectator in recent years. Perhaps I will sponsor a new set of whites for the first XI instead when I get back on my feet.

Gabe insisted I needed counselling. And he wanted to know a lot more about Geena Dale. I told him all he needed to know, including information I had gleaned through an unofficial request from an old friend on the force that her criminal record was slim: she had been arrested with several others on a drugs charge when she was barely twenty - apparently she had made matters slightly worse by resisting arrest through persistent use of her teeth. I tried to reinforce my belief in her. I suppose I had made a leap of faith which he was loath to follow. He couldn't accept that I knew my own mind. I suppose he must have thought that I was having some kind of mid-life crisis.

THIRTEEN

The scene plays in Donald Percey's car, parked unlit on a lonely forest track in the darkness of a chilly night in May. A second car approaches slowly from the rear, crackling over the stones, stops directly behind his and its headlights close down. Within seconds Geena Dale is sitting next to him in his passenger seat, pulling the door firmly shut against the cold, rubbing her hands one against the other, and Don flicks a switch to prevent the courtesy light from dimming out.

"So, what's the matter, Geena?" he says. "Are you in trouble? You're trembling."

"Am I? It's the chill. Should've brought a scarf. I'm sorry to drag you out here. It's been a bit of a rush. No, I'm not in any trouble. Well, not really. Not the sort of trouble *you* mean…"

"What sort of trouble do *you* mean?"

Don has turned his body awkwardly in his seat to address her, but the woman remains face forward to the windscreen, as prim as she might be on a church pew.

"It's nothin' we can't get out of. *I* can't get out of."

"Geena, what's going on? What are we doing here sitting in the dark?"

"I'm sorry."

"Don't apologise, just tell me what I can do to help and then we can both go home."

"This is a bit embarrassin," she says in a whisper, clearing her throat before continuing.

"Just tell me," he demands.

She is still talking to the dashboard, twisting her earlobe with the fingers of her left hand:

"You know you offered me some money in the pub back-along?"

"How could I forget? *Some* money? It was more than just *some* money."

"An' how I told you to stick it, yeah?"

"Yes, whatever it was you said, I got the message."

"Well…,"

He can see how uncomfortable she is, he can hear the torment in her voice.

"What? Just say…"

"Well…, can I, can I change my mind?"

"Change your mind?"

"Please? Please, Don…"

"You need money?"

"Just a little. I hate askin'. If the offer is still there?"

Don has more surprise in his voice than he is feeling; he had seen this coming but had not known when.

"Yes, I suppose."

"Don, I don't need your thousands," she says quietly, now angling her body slightly towards his and tilting her head to catch his eye. "But I do need some cash and I don't know who else I can ask. Just a loan… I'll pay it back…"

"I don't do loans, Geena," he cuts in. "I told you that before. You won't pay me back. You won't have to." He is genuinely excited now, a batsman in form facing an over from a nervous slow bowler. "My feelings might be bruised but they haven't changed since the last time we talked about all this."

Geena sighs with relief, taking a deep breath before pressing on:

"It's my car," she says, looking over her shoulder. "To start with, anyway. The door seal leaks; if it pisses down I get dripped on. It failed its MOT last week: brakes, lights, tyres, nightmare. They reckon it'd be over £500 to fix it. More than the bloody thing's worth. An' I just don't have it, Don, that kind of money. An' I can't manage without a car. How will I get in to work, into town? The buses are rubbish, there's none after dark, I just don't know what…".

"Okay, stop, stop. I'll pay for your car. Relax."

"I hate askin'."

"Don't worry."

She leans over suddenly and takes him by surprise by kissing him on the cheek.

"You're a lifesaver, Don Percey!"

"Am I?" he asks, a little embarrassed.

"Yes, you are. Please don't tell Polo or Sharky or anyone else, will you, though?"

"Sharky? I've hardly exchanged two words with him. Why would I even think of telling him anything?"

"I just don't want him to know. He doesn't need to know, yeah?"

"Of course not."

"Right."

"How would he react if he found out? If he found out that you've been accepting money from someone else? Someone like me?"

"He'd probably freak out," she says with a hollow laugh. "He's a jealous one, he is. It wouldn't be about the money, though, more about me sneakin' out in the dark behind his back with another man…"

"We're not sneaking around…"

"Yeah, we are! That exactly what we're doin'! Well, what *I'm* doin'. An' he'd put two an' two together… and, you know, he'd be thinkin'… money for sex, sex for money… in his head."

"Would he?"

"Yeah, an' he can get a bit lairy."

"Can he?"

"Yeah, but he's never been like that with me. He's a pussy cat. Bit different with guys, though."

"He treats you okay?"

"What do you mean?"

"You know what I mean, does he treat you well?"

"Some of the time, I suppose."

"Only some of the time?"

"Most of the time."

"Most of the time? Really? Not *all* the time?"

"Most of the time. That's good enough, ain't it?"

"Is it?"

"It's good enough for me. Good enough for most, I reckon. That's what everyone has to settle for, yeah?

"I don't know, Geena. I don't know. You may be right."

"I'm right, course I am. I know men. *Most of the time*, that's pretty good. Good enough. Anyway, where's this goin', Don?"

"Nowhere, really. I was just curious. Nosey, I suppose. I'm sorry."

"Forget it."

Don straightens up in his seat.

"So, okay, we keep this to ourselves."

"Yeah, please. We do."

There is a moment's silence between them. She is wearing a tatty denim jacket over a strappy top so thin that the line of her bra beneath it is perfectly clear. Her cotton skirt has ridden above her knees which are six inches apart, no longer covered in gooseflesh, her right brushing against the gearstick. Ever the detective, Don has noticed all these fine details.

She has more to say:

"An' there's the oil bill."

"The oil bill?"

"The last six months, over the winter. I've put it to one side, tried to forget about it. But I can't get close to payin' it this time. Benefits only take me so far, Don, you know. I 'm really strugglin', feel like I'm sinkin'..."

She is trembling again, suddenly close to tears, and Don knows it.

"Hey, come on. No blubbing."

He moves almost imperceptively into a position to receive her if she is inclined to fall into his arms like her troubled son had done a few weeks earlier. He will hold her, comfort her, feel the warmth of her body against his chest, stroke her hair, wipe away the tears from her soft cheeks. But Geena doesn't fall into his arms. She breathes deeply, sniffs once or twice and pulls herself upright in her seat.

"I'm okay," she mumbles.

"You sure?"

"Yeah."

"Okay. No tears, eh?"

She pulls forward the sun visor, looking for the vanity mirror where she checks her eyes and cheeks for smudges in the light of a single yellow bulb.

"God, I look awful."

"Don't be silly."

"I do."

Don lets it ride, then starts again:

"You know you really should have listened to me properly the last time and given me a bit more of a chance to explain myself..."

"I panicked."

"And I was clumsy."

"I won't panic again."

"That's because you know what to expect."

"An' I've had time to think about it properly."

"You've been thinking about it, about what I offered?"

"Yeah, I have," she says, turning her head to face his with a smile. "An' I was hasty. An' if you can forgive me, forgive me for bein' such a stroppy cow, so ungrateful, then..."

"I forgive you," he says, returning her smile. "Of course I do."

"So, you'll help?"

"I said I would. Of course I'll help. It's what I wanted to do before and I still do."

"Oh, thank you, thank you, thank you!"

And now her smile is transformed from mechanical to a natural beam in which her eyes catch the light and sparkle.

She is ready to reach out to embrace him but is reined in by the sudden sound of her mobile's ringtone.

"Who's this?" she says, pulling the phone from her jacket pocket. "Oh, it's just Roz."

"Roz?"

"From number three."

"The girl with the piercings?"

"Yeah, Roz. She said she'd ring when Amber got back."

In the minute or so that the phone conversation lasts, Don takes out his cheque book, scribbles on the first open page and tears it out.

"She was only up the village at a friend's. I keep better tabs on Amber. I let the boys run a bit wild, I admit. They used to stay out late, even after dark at her age. I tell her it's 'cos she's a girl. She says it's not fair, but I think they're more, you know, girls, risky, don't you, Don?"

"What?"

"Girls. I worry about her more. You hear about pervs, don't you?"

"Vulnerable."

"Yeah, exactly. You must know all about it, bein' a gavver an' all."

"Well, boys are at risk too, but statistically, yes, you'd be right. I'm glad Amber got home safely."

"Thanks. An' for the money. Don, I'm so grateful. There must be somethin' I can do to repay you…"

"No strings. We said so last time, and I meant it. You owe me nothing, Geena."

"No strings. Okay. You're the boss."

"I'm the boss."

"Yeah, you really are."

"Right, I'm the boss and I've just made a decision." A sense of purpose is returning to his voice as he passes the strip of paper into her fingers. "I've written you a cheque right here and now for £10,000. Okay? And when Polo goes up to Green Bank in September and you'll need to buy a new uniform and stacks of school stuff, I'm going to give you a second cheque for the same amount…"

"But Don, that's too much…"

"Listen, Geena, we've been here before. And this time you're not running away. I'll lock you in the car if I have to. This is *my* deal. You've asked me for help and I'm glad you did. I'm *flattered* that you did. And so this is how I'll help you: £10,000 now, £10,000 in September, and £20,000 a year for the next nine years."

"Twenty?" she splutters. "That's double what you said last time! It's crazy!"

"I know. It *is* crazy. But the difference is that I get an even bigger buzz giving it to you, twice the buzz, and this time you're simply not allowed to refuse it!"

I was in the minibus, travelling at top speed over empty wasteland, bouncing in and out of deep channels in the rutted tracks, kicking up dust and dirt into the dark grey sky, engine grumbling up to a rocky crest then screaming on the downhill. My heart was pounding, my teeth on edge, my left hand gripping the door, my right sliding along the dashboard as we hurtled into another crazy double bend. By my side and with his hands tight to the wheel, *my* wheel, face frozen in an expression of manic excitement, pushing the tired old Transit to its outer limits was Alec Otterbridge, king of the rallycross, prince of all plumbers, cuckold of the world wide web.

I heard voices behind me, coming from Rita's seat, but not hers. Each time I took my eyes off the cracked windscreen to turn and see who was talking it was a different voice, a different face. I saw Tommy Kremitz, Kermit, in distress, struggling to take off his seat belt, gasping for breath. *Use your inhaler*, I shouted, but he just shook his head and called back to me: *It's broken, it's on the floor somewhere,* and then, in a panic, *I have to see my father! I have to!*

Onward we drove, crashing over the moonscape, aiming for some dot on the jagged horizon. I turned again, hearing the voice of Malcolm Ashworth: he was lolling in Rita's seat, in his Batman tee-shirt and cut-off jeans, smoking a joint. *Wanna drag?* he asked. *You can't smoke in here,* I called. *I can smoke where I want*, he replied with a grin. *Wherever I want.*

Then it was Coppinger's turn, there right behind me in a white England rugby shirt, several sizes too small. *Don't worry, Donny, we'll nail the bastard for you*, he said, over and over again until the roar of the engine drowned him out.

Sometimes pierced Roz appeared, nothing to say, fiddling with an earring and smirking at me.

Outside it was always dry and dusty but sometimes rain poured in, inexplicably, on to my shoulder through a damaged door seal. And always Otterbridge at the wheel, flashing me a snarl, piloting the bus as though we were being chased by the hounds of hell.

Even dreams?

Especially dreams.

Last night he took it to the extreme and then beyond, racing out over the horizon, accelerating towards the very edge of a vast pit, a deep, open quarry as wide as a great river canyon. I was frantic, shouting to him to stop, to turn back, desperately trying to drown out the passengers bouncing around behind me.

I can smoke where I want!

Wordless smirks from the piercings.

We'll nail the bastard for you, Donny!

I have to see my father! I have to!

There were screams of delirium from the driver's throat, and from mine only strained shrieks of terror. And suddenly the bus took off like a bird, a flightless, spastic bird, and I was falling in space, air beneath the wheels, emptiness thumping into my stomach, assaulted by the cold slap of nausea.

I woke up in an icy, shivering sweat, fists clenched tight, bedclothes in disarray, and found Juliet mopping my face with a flannel. It took me half a minute to gather myself before I could even try to return her smile. *That was an exciting one, she was saying*, but I had no words to respond. *You were calling for Carole*, she said. *Just now, you were calling for Carole.* I slowly understood what she was telling me. *Was I?* I mumbled eventually.

Was I?

I remember very little about the Easter holidays. That time is still just a blur. I didn't see Geena Dale for two weeks and that was a blessing. Everything was still too raw.

Back on the school run there was just a reprise of our trivial, throwaway conversations whenever we met, Polo between us, the innocent child. Innocent is the wrong word: it was at about this time that he was excluded from school for two days after telling one of his teachers to fuck off.

So it was with genuine surprise that I read a text message she sent to my mobile one evening when I was at home sitting in front of the TV. (Of course, I had given her my number weeks before). She wanted - needed? - to speak to me, in private like before, but not in *that pub*. Too many bad memories? She wanted to meet in a hikers' car park by the roadside, I knew it, on the edge of the plantations, a few miles beyond her village. At nine o'clock. I remember the details. Nine o'clock. Late. A guarantee of darkness.

You must come. Even if you can't come don't text me back. So you must come.

I can recall this subterfuge as clearly as the meeting at The Royal Oak. I arrived at the spot first. The last glimmers of light in the sky had long faded. A three-quarter moon hung passively above the tree tops. There was another car parked up twenty yards away, no lights on, but it was not Geena's. It was a pick-up, and in it a man was smoking with his window wound down. I remember smelling the burning tobacco mingling with the light scent of pine dew. I had no idea who he was. He seemed wrapped up in his own thoughts - was he reading, or texting? - but when Geena did arrive, I suggested she follow me and we drove away from the car park and edged down a loggers' track a hundred yards or so into the blackness of the forest.

An owl called out as I opened my passenger door to let her in. She was wearing a heavy, cheap perfume, and in the dark, in the stillness, we sat and we quietly talked. Geena was desperate for money, and this time she would take anything I offered. No hesitation. No reservations. It took courage to ask, I acknowledge that, and in her flustered, roundabout way she was begging for a second chance, and I was excited once again at the prospect of bailing her out. I hadn't stopped wanting to do it just because she'd knocked me back a month before, but to be honest, I didn't expect her to change her mind so soon.

Was it her closeness to me, just inches between us, a delicious prickle of anticipation, the whispered urgency in her voice, the heady thrill of sharing an intimacy - was it all of this that made me double up the offer of money? Was it the adrenalin of the moment, the feeling, like teetering on a cliff top, of trembling on the very edge of a great act? Whatever, in the soft yellow glow of the courtesy light I wrote Geena Dale a cheque for £10,000 and then, in the next breath, spilling out of my mouth came the promise of *two hundred* thousand over ten years. Madness? I don't know. But I felt deliciously alive in a way I had never felt before. An exhilaration was pulsing through me from my heart to my fingertips.

Am I being honest when I say that the thrill was in no way sexual? She spoke of sex. *Money for sex, sex for money.* It was what her boyfriend would think if he ever found out. And she kissed me on the cheek, not out of gratitude, I think, but out of relief. For me it was not about sex or even the prospect of sex with Geena. But as I drove home after we parted, I admit that my mind did wander into a forbidden place where she lay soft and open for my pleasure. Nevertheless, hesitating to walk that quivering tightrope, I couldn't stop myself wondering, to my disgrace, just how *hygienic* it might be. And it was as inevitable as it was shameful that once back home, within a minute or two of soaking in deep, hot water, luxuriated with the last drops of Carole's *Fleurs de Provence* bath oil, I quickly released myself in fevered, angry pulses which left me feeling light-headed and inept.

FOURTEEN

The scene plays in Don Percey's home, by the French windows which are open to the fragile warmth of early summer. Father and son are in quiet conversation, the younger man's voice the first to grow distinct:

"I thought that Mum would have loved a rose like that. You used to have a pale yellow one down by the greenhouse, didn't you?"

"Years ago, we did, yeah," says Don, stepping into the room, dusting off his hands. "With a beautiful scent. It had a girl's name... I've forgotten. No, it died a long time ago, sadly. Anyway, yours is a perfect replacement. I'll put it in the ground later, when you've gone. There's a space I have in mind over in that right-hand border. It'll look fabulous, especially in a year or two. Thanks, Gabe."

He is about to sit down, but thinks to ask:

"Will you have a cup of tea, coffee?"

"No, thanks, Dad. I'm not stopping. I just came round to deliver the bush, and this..."

Gabe fishes out a folded card from his jacket pocket and hands it to Don.

"What's this then?" asks his father.

"It's from Ollie. Open it."

Don opens the card and reads aloud the words printed in his grandchild's deliberate hand:

"*Dear Grandad. Please come to a party for my 7th birthday! at my house on Fridday 17th of June. after school. dont forget! love from Oliver X*"

"Lovely! The seventeenth, that's next week, isn't it? Yes, absolutely. Tell him I'll be there." He turns back to look again at the front of the card: a drawing of a cake and seven wobbly candles in bold primary colours. "He's quite an artist."

"Yes, he's got an eye for a line," says Gabe with a grin.

"I'd love to come, of course. I'll be around after I've done the afternoon run. Some time after half past five, I expect."

"Right. Great. I'll tell him you accept. There'll be a dozen or so other kids from his class there, so don't expect just a quiet drink…"

"As if! I'm not so old that I've forgotten what children's parties are like!"

"Oh, it's been a while, Dad."

Gabe is making as if to leave when Don asks:

"How's Grace?"

"Grace?"

"Yes, your wife. How is she?"

"Well, yes, that's the third reason I've come round, really."

"Oh?"

Gabe has been toying with the idea of ducking this part of the conversation, but he realises it has already begun. He chooses a seat by the windows and Don instinctively follows his lead.

"It's just that I wanted…," starts Gabe, "well, *she* wanted to apologise for how she, how *we* reacted when you told us about Mum's money. Well, *your* money. The money you said you were giving, you know, to Geena Dale."

Don listens without comment as his son staggers on:

"She's sorry for what she said, and how it's caused an atmosphere these past few weeks."

Don has no wish to make this any harder for his son.

"Fine."

"She's not been herself, Grace hasn't. You've probably noticed."

"It's fine, honestly. Forget it. It's done."

"No, seriously," adds Gabe, fixing his father with a look of sadness and fatigue. "She's been depressed. Edgy. Irritable. We both have, really, but especially Gracie."

"What do you mean?"

"It's this baby thing, Dad," he sighs. "You know. You know we've been trying for ages now for another…"

"I thought you'd settled on one. On Oliver."

"Yes, well, it's looking as if we've no choice. We've been trying for over two years and had all the tests done." He pauses; it was always much easier talking about this stuff with his mother. "Grace has become morbidly obsessed with hormone levels," he stumbles on. "We're in an endless wait for IVF. Because we're not childless we're last in the queue. In other words, it'll never happen…"

"I'm sorry," says Don in little more than a whisper. "Your mum told me you were hoping for a second child, but that was a year ago now, at least, and I thought… well, I just thought you'd changed your mind, or else…"

He suddenly has an idea:

"But… couldn't you go private, you know, for the IVF?"

"Private? That'll cost the earth, and there's still no guarantee."

Realising where this could lead, he interrupts himself:

"Oh, hang on, no, Dad! No, this is not what I meant. It's not a plea for funds for private treatment. You mustn't think that. God, I'm only telling you because of how Grace has been. Now I wish I'd said nothing. Please don't think I've come round here with a begging bowl…"

"No, I'm not saying that…"

"Dad, it's *our* problem. *We'll* deal with it. I just needed to explain about Grace…"

"I have the money."

"You're not listening to me!"

"Alright. Fine. Calm down, son."

Suddenly Rina pads softly into the room, gives Gabe an up-and-down look, chooses to sit with Don and springs up lightly on to his lap. Both men watch her and smile.

"I just wanted to tell you that's why my wife has been short with you. Well, with everybody. You should have heard her with the secretary at Ollie's school!" he adds with a hard-bitten laugh.

"Is she on drugs now?" asks Don.

"She's on fertility drugs, yeah. Since March."

"Oh. Well, you never know…"

"No. You never know."

Gabe stands up and turns to gaze out into the garden.

"At least you have Oliver," says Don, offering a smile of support.

"Yes, yes we do. And he's an angel. We are blessed. We shouldn't be greedy. Some people have none. I've told her that one can be perfect."

"You were an only child," says Don. "You turned out okay…"

Gabe looks back into the room and smiles at his father, who is gently stroking the kitten's head.

"That cat loves you, doesn't she?"

"Yeah, I think she does."

He tickles her fluffy neck and she flashes a soft paw at his hand.

"Thanks for telling me about Grace. It's moments like this that we need your mother back amongst us."

Don moves to stand up, Rina jumps away, and he steps forward to put a hand on his son's arm. Gabe looks up.

"I should have told you before."

"You told me now. That's fine. And give my love to Grace."

"I will."

The two men embrace briefly. Gabe takes a deep breath, wanting to draw a line.

"So, I'll see you again soon, Dad."

"You're off?"

"Yes, I said I'd get straight back."

"So, it'll be next week, then."

"Yes, next week, if not before."

"At the party!"

"At the party, of course. Next Friday… ice cream and fizzy drinks all round!"

I was saddened but not surprised by the way in which the business with Geena Dale had become a taboo subject in conversations between my son and me. I tried to understand his point of view, but I suppose my own vision at the time was blurred by a touch of vertigo. Nevertheless, once bitten, twice shy: I was unwilling to stoke up the fire by justifying myself over and over, and, needless to say, I kept my promise to Geena to double the size of my ten-year gift to myself. Gabe knew that I was not to be diverted and he had reluctantly accepted that. At least we had not revisited the subject, and a kind of uneasy truce took hold in the following weeks.

A reconciliation of sorts took place on the anniversary of Carole's accident. Gabe called round alone with a rose bush for the garden. I was genuinely touched. It was a gesture which I did really appreciate. Carole was a fan of roses, especially yellow, cream, peach-coloured ones, but they never seemed to flourish for very long in our chalky soil. I think she realised she was fighting a losing battle with nature, but as soon as one bush died, she'd feed up the earth and dig in a new one, ever the optimist. As soon as Gabe left I did the same, setting to work in a sunny spot with a spade, a large bag of fertilizer, a barrow load of compost and plenty of water. I remember it was a slightly hazardous task and I should have worn gloves: the thorns were as sharp as piranha teeth and my fingers were covered in nicks, but the blood spilt will be worth it. The new bush will need some care as it was already budding: a floribunda, the colour of butter. I hope it hasn't been neglected while I've been in hospital.

Gabe had also come round to let me into a confidence. Proud parents of an enchanting son, he and Grace were nevertheless numbingly frustrated by failure, month after month after month, to produce for him a little brother or sister. I remember thinking when he had left that they were young, they still had time on their side.

When Carole and I were in India we were allowed to visit a school for orphans. She had been teaching nine- and ten-year-olds for a year or so already, and her functional role and sense of professional distance must have kept her own maternal instincts at bay. However, after an hour touring the crowded little classrooms of this orphanage, full of lively, noisy but cheerful, polite, *engaging* children, something inside her melted and the pangs for involvement, for closeness, indeed for motherhood grew unstoppable. We talked about it for hours on the long train journey north back to Delhi. I remember the huge orange sun slowly sinking, turning a smouldering fiery red, singeing the horizon as it slipped elegantly away. Its warm glow streamed in on our side of the rickety carriage, bathing Carole's tanned face, illuminating the passion in her eyes. She became ever more animated; both of us were intoxicated by our plans, our hopes of having lots of children, boys and girls, girls and boys; we had love in abundance, plenty of affection to go round, masses for everyone.

As things turned out, we were thwarted in our plans to have a large family. I could relate entirely to the pain that Gabe and Grace were feeling. It was a difficult time for us, of course, but we got through it. The disappointment faded slowly and we counted our blessings to have a healthy son. If anything it brought us closer together as a couple, and as a threesome.

I've been wondering about Carole. She was a compassionate woman. In her working life she had treated both children and their parents who had hit hard times with kindness. I know there had been times when she had supplemented the funds for subsidising poorer children's participation on school outings from her own pocket. She had a big heart. Would she have seen in Geena Dale a cause worth supporting? Morally? Emotionally? Financially? Would she congratulate me on my altruism, my philanthropic instincts? Or would she think I had lost my mind to an indulgent whim and my heart to an irresponsible freeloader with a pretty face?

FIFTEEN

The scene plays by the same minibus, parked by No.1 The Pavilions. Polo Dale steps off the bus, ignores his mother, runs past her across the grass, throws his bag and jumper to the ground and barges into the house. Pink-haired Geena Dale watches him disappear inside before calling out to him:

"Hey, a hello would be nice, yeah?"

"He's been in a good mood all this week," Rita is saying, through the open door of the bus, "but got into a grump when we stopped for the rainbow back there."

"You stopped for what?"

"The rainbow. Look," she adds, pointing, "you can still see a bit of it from here. If you look over those roofs. See."

From his driver's seat Don Percey turns back to explain, as if accepting some sort of blame:

"It was my idea. As we were coming down the long hill from Reece's village, it was bright sunlight on the left and rain clouds on the right. Extraordinary. And within seconds, *as I predicted*, there was the most brilliant rainbow, actually a *double* rainbow. Perfectly clear."

"Don got a bit overexcited," says Rita, laughing.

"It *was* pretty spectacular, admit it…"

"So he stopped the bus in the lane and them that wanted to

could get out and admire the view…"

"The full view. No use through a little side window."

Geena gives them both a look of disbelief, then a tolerant smile:

"You got the kids off the bus, in the rain, to look at a rainbow?"

"A double rainbow," Don insists. "And it wasn't actually raining where we were."

"Just as well, you daft thing…"

"Anyway," says Rita, "Don said it looked as though it ended right over these houses, right here. Actually it did."

"I said something about a pot of gold at the end of the rainbow, right in your back garden. It was just a joke." "Polo stayed in his seat and said that pot of gold stuff, *that's just another grown-up lie*. He hasn't said another word to nobody these past five minutes."

Geena looks to see if the boy has come back outside, then sighs.

"Never mind," she says, "He does get depressed sometimes. It don't take much. Over the silliest things. I can't work out his moods. He can be a nightmare…"

"But, as I said, Geena, he's been great all week," says Rita, trying to cheer things up again; after all, it *is* Friday. "Really good company, hasn't he, Don? Talkin' about the Big School. It won't be long now, will it? After the summer. Just a few more weeks left on the bus with me, and he'll be gone."

"That's part of the problem, Reet, I think. He's fed up where he is, we all know that, but it's a big step. It is, it's a big step, ain't it? I remember Angelo going on backalong, he never settled. Polo's worried about how he'll fit in, I can tell. We've talked about it a bit. New friends, new teachers, new rules an' all."

"He'll be fine," Don chips in.

"Have you got him his uniform yet?" asks Rita.

"No, not yet. I'll get him fixed up in the holidays."

"It's an expense, though, isn't it? All new stuff too but…"

"I'll manage."

"Of course you will," says Don, with the slightest of involuntary glances towards Geena. "You'll be fine. It's a priority. A new school, a new start, he needs the best chance you can give him."

"Don't worry, he'll get the best chance. Course, he's a priority. Course he is."

She turns to shout to the boy:

"Polo!"

She walks away from the door and towards her son who is back outside already, two doors down, playing with the neighbours' dogs.

"Polo, come here, you little rogue," she shouts. "Come and give your mum a big hug!"

As she skips round the front of the bus she winks at Don and, in the same instant, blows him a little kiss, before she's away, striding off:

"Come here, Polo Dale! Fish fingers for tea, my lovely little boy! Have a nice weekend, Reet! Be good!"

COUNTY HOSPITAL

This morning I saw in one of the hospital corridors a woman in a wheelchair with her face bandaged. I have no idea why only her pale blue eyes were visible and it was hard to say whether it was pain or hope I could see behind their flickering. The sight of the anonymous patient reminded me of the morning, not too long ago, when I punched a lady in the face. Not deliberately, you will understand. I found myself sharing a lane in the swimming pool with the woman ploughing up and back, head down like me, in imprecise versions of front crawl. One or both of us must have strayed from the designated protocol and in the inevitable collision, often no worse than a brush of a leg, involved my flailing arm crashing into her face with some force. We both stopped in mid-length, coughing and splashing around anxiously, me full of apologies and the poor woman shocked by the assault. *Is my nose bleeding?* she asked. *I'm sure my nose is bleeding!* Luckily it was not. When we ended up in the shallows together a few minutes later the tension had eased and we shared a forced laugh and I was forgiven. Even behind her goggles I could see that she had a pretty face and a generous smile.

You hear about romances starting in such inauspicious ways and I have to admit my mind raced into overdrive during the next few days, hoping that she would be at the pool at the same time the following week. Sure enough, she was and this time I was already in the water and could watch from a distance as she lowered her slim suited body gracefully into the shallow end. As usual the pool was fairly busy and perhaps sensibly she chose to swim in a different lane to mine but she spotted me a little later, waved and smiled. I began to wonder if it was a *Hi, I'm available* smile, and immediately lost count of the number of lengths I had swum. As discreetly as I could, I kept my eye on her and timed my exit to coincide with hers, hoping to bump into her in the foyer later and maybe suggest a coffee. All of which happened except for the coffee. Out in the reception area I caught up with her only to find her in the arms of a boyfriend. On their way out, she noticed me and smiled again. It was the same enigmatic smile, but less of a *Hi, I'm available* one and more of the type that said *Hi, I'm happy to be in a loving and fulfilling relationship with this gorgeous guy who has spent the last fifty minutes in the gym upstairs pushing weights.*

At the beginning of the summer term I joined an evening class for Tourists' German, having bitten the bullet and booked myself on an eight-day Rhineland cruise. Gabriel had bullied me into a holiday, and for years I had neglected a seed of interest in the area which had been planted by a teacher from my old school days who was originally from Cologne. I was no great linguist but he was sympathetic, supportive and as such was quite a rarity. I was placed in a German set at the age of eleven and tried to come to terms with a language where all the verbs seemed to be shunted to the end of the sentence like a pile-up on the Autobahn. In my hands they sounded like the ammunition of a Gestapo officer with a nervous stammer. But five years later and at least I did know what a verb was: regular and irregular, transitive and intransitive, auxiliary and modal, a blitz of tenses, infinitives, subjunctives and even the neglected gerund. I knew them all: all their functions and amazing super-powers. Sadly I couldn't be bothered to learn enough vocabulary. And vocabulary, really, is all you need to get by in any language, isn't it? Vocabulary, a few facial expressions and a bit of cheek. So, not enough vocabulary, not enough marks for an O Level pass. Not even close. *Es war meine Schuld.*

Forty years on and I found myself in a class of six, including two attractive middle-aged sisters whose flirting during pair-work is borderline criminal; or perhaps it is my imagination. Either way our noses are kept to the grindstone by Frieda Clipperton, or Frau Clipperton as she prefers, who has no truck with veering away from her lesson plans and treats the ladies' sniggers at the mention of *oral practice* with disdain. As indeed she should. Her husband and young family are new to the county, having bought a pair of cottages in one of the nicer villages to have renovated, rethatched and knocked into one substantial *Doppelhaus*, as she calls it. Her husband, a commodities broker in the City, still spends much of his week in their other home in Essex. *Juggling two homes is such a trial,* she said, but was she expecting sympathy? In one lesson she tried to explain exactly what her husband did for his well-rewarded living, starting off in German but then having to retrace her steps in English, which actually did little to dispel the confusion in the classroom.

My long hospital stay has meant that I have missed my Rhineland cruise after all; it sailed one day last week. Gabe has been chasing up the company to see if I'm due some kind of refund.

The early weeks of summer offered a new face to the lanes along which our bus travelled, the wide views of open fields and farmland now hidden behind abundant hedge growth, rich, bursting patterns of green, tree branches weighed down, suddenly, or so it seemed, with clusters of shimmering new leaves. Spindly ranks of cow parsley stretched to the sky, tall stalks bending in the warm breeze, preening like party girls, their fluffy milk-white heads bobbing above the straggly grasses and soft young ferns, above the eager nettles and arching canes of bramble, above the tangles of wild wispy weeds, watery yellow and dusty pink, which hugged the scuffed edges of the roadside.

Although The Pavilions offered few signs of life at eight o'clock most mornings, by the afternoons in June we often arrived to find what looked like the remnants of an outdoor party. The front patches of scarred grass were littered with abandoned toys, food wrappers and beer cans. Young children with dirty faces might be chasing each other around a rough arc of cheap camping chairs in which any combination of residents could be dozing, smoking or listening to the music echoing from inside somebody's kitchen. There would always be at least two mongrels running around in circles and a carelessly parked car which made my job of manoeuvring the minibus all the more difficult. One day, a warm day of bright sunshine, a child of about five with a shaven head, a little imp of a boy in nothing but his underpants, attacked the bus with a series of water bombs - balloons he had filled up and stored in a bucket until we appeared in the lane. I wondered what the noise was as the first deceptively heavy thud hit the rear door, and then another exploded at the side window, startling Rita. When I looked out to tell him to stop, he off-loaded a couple more, squealed with delight, made a show to me of his middle finger and skipped into his house for cover. A group of little girls watched and giggled. I think one of them must have been Amber.

As usual it was never easy to guess who would be at No.1 to take Polo off our hands. Angelo was around quite a lot, I remember; sometimes with his baby daughter but I never saw the teenage mother. He remained morose with me - and with Rita too, for that matter. Life really did seem to offer little joy to him; smiling was what other people did. As a compensation cigarettes (both tobacco and otherwise) and cheap cider never seemed too far away.

If Geena was at home to meet us she was generally in good spirits. She'd been offered a Saturday shift at the cheese factory and the little grumbles to Rita over money worries had dried up. She readily involved me in her conversation and she spoke to me casually, flippantly, as though our meeting in the woods had never happened. Once she blew me a fleeting kiss. I don't think she meant anything by it but she made a point of making sure Rita saw nothing. I was intrigued by it all the way home: a throwaway, meaningless kiss like the x people stick on the end of their text messages, a light-hearted gesture, no more than a ghost of a kiss, a fluffy sign of fondness, dismissively playful, as far from an expression of desire as you could possibly get.

Geena wasn't looking forward to the school holidays - *How am I goin' to cope with them two under my feet all day long?* - but the sigh came with a smile which shone through her exasperation. And, we learned, she was planning a little holiday for them all, somewhere on the Isle of Wight where Sharky had a pal who knew someone who owned a caravan. In spite of this being what seemed to me the flakiest of plans, she was genuinely excited. *Polo will love it. A proper holiday before he goes to Green Bank.* It made me smile inside to see her so ditzy and so happy.

And yes, Sharky was definitely still on the scene. He it was who now occasionally collected Polo off the minibus, usually with a dimp between his teeth and in the scruffiest of clothes. There was a week or so when he disappeared (Rita had been told that he and Geena had had a massive row and she'd kicked him out), but by the end of June his dirtbike was regularly back outside the kitchen window.

He was about thirty, at a guess, overweight but tall enough to carry it. His long, straggly black hair and halfway beard enclosed a flabby face whose eyes, watery blue and tiny, were slightly squinty. He was a casual labourer, working demolition sites by choice, apparently, and his well-defined muscles were decorated with a range of tattoos which were given full show by his choice of armless tee-shirts. Nobody seemed to know his real name. If he spoke to me it was no more than to say thanks for driving Polo home. Thanks was not a word I had ever heard on the lips of Malcolm Ashworth, and so in spite of my instinctive reservations I was already more favourably disposed towards him than I had been to Polo's absent father.

One afternoon, as we arrived at Geena's house, I noticed that Sharky was cleaning his scrambler on the grass outside the front door. He had two plastic buckets, a sponge, tins of polish and a pile of rags lined up as if he were halfway through a very thorough job. I heard him shout to an inquisitive dog sniffing the rags to fuck off. He nodded as he saw me, and then as I swung the bus round to reverse into position, he disappeared inside the house, to emerge seconds later wearing, over his grey tee-shirt, what looked like a brand new black leather bomber jacket with a sheepskin collar. Before Polo had got down off the bus, Sharky strode up to my window, lifted his sunglasses, turned up the jacket collar and, in something of an exaggerated performance through the glass as if I might be deaf, mouthed the familiar but now unsettling words: *thank you*. He waited for my reaction, and seeing only an uncertain half-smile, he turned away with a grin and resumed his chore.

I thought about this incident all evening. I didn't know the man. I was unaware of his mannerisms, his quirks, his patterns of behaviour. Was I imagining a conspiracy that wasn't real? Was he having a bit of fun, showing off a new jacket like he was one of the great rock stars? Was he even slightly unhinged? Or was an under-employed sponger helping himself to a share of the money I had given, *secretly,* to a woman who happened to be, for the moment at least, his latest girlfriend? In which case he had stolen it, or Geena Dale had told him the truth. Our truth. Or had she bought it for him as a present, as a thank you for being such a brilliant lover? But no, I was getting ahead of myself. This was nonsense. She had no reason to tell him about the money; she had virtually sworn me to secrecy. And, after all, what does a leather jacket cost, even a good one: £200? £300 at the most? He was earning, he could afford it perhaps, a one-off luxury, a little treat. I was unnerved briefly, I admit, but was able to rationalise everything pretty quickly, and with things back in their proper perspective, I put the episode firmly to the back of my mind.

SIXTEEN

The scene plays in Don's home, in the lounge occupied by three generations of Perceys. It is the excitable voice of the youngest, the boy Oliver, squatting on the sofa cuddling Rina, which is heard:

"Grandad, do you want the good news or the bad news first?"

Don pulls a theatrically gloomy face:

"Oh, this again!"

And Gabe, genuinely concerned, cuts in:

"Ollie… what are you going to say?"

"I'm going to tell Grandad our secret."

"*Our* secret? Ollie, you know what we said. It's *Mummy's* secret. And we promised we'd *keep* it a secret, didn't we?"

"But I want to tell Grandad. That's okay, isn't it, Daddy? Mummy won't mind if I tell Grandad."

"Okay," says his father, sighing then smiling. "Okay, but nobody else. Nobody at school, alright?"

The boy is ever more animated, he cannot hold in the good news for much longer:

"Yes, nobody else. Grandad, guess what!"

"And definitely nobody at your swim club," adds Gabe.

"Grandad!" the boy insists, "Guess what!"

"What, Oliver? What?"

"Mummy's having a baby!"

"Is she?"

Don is astounded, he looks back to Gabe to check. Gabe is nodding and grinning like a man who knows he has just scored the winning goal in a cup final. Don's face breaks into the broadest of smiles and he strides over, almost leaps over, to where his son is sitting:

"Well, this is fantastic news! Really fantastic! Wonderful!"

The kitten decides it is time to leave the room. She hops off Oliver's lap and dances into the kitchen. Meanwhile Don is vigorously shaking Gabe's hand:

"Congratulations, son! You must be over the moon!"

"Well, that's an understatement." Gabe's eyes have begun to moisten and he checks his breathing to add: "Grace is just so relieved. Well, both of us are. We're absolutely thrilled."

"Mummy is going to get fat first," states Oliver.

"Is she?"

"Before the baby comes."

"Then she'll get thin again, won't she?" confirms his father.

"Yes. Then she'll get thin again. Grandad, aren't you going to ask me?"

"Ask you what?"

"Ask me," he says, beginning to giggle, "ask me what the bad news is?"

"Oh, right. Yes, of course, Oliver. What, please tell me, is the bad news?"

The boy, bursting into a fit of giggles, eventually responds:

"I… I forgot!"

"You forgot? Again?"

"It's his latest joke, Dad," says Gabe, shaking his head in mock annoyance.

"I forgot!" he repeats, rolling off the sofa onto the carpet.

"Well, you can come again if you only bring me good news!"

The boy picks himself up and scampers into the kitchen:

"Rina! Where are you, Rina? Come here, you silly cat!"

The two men watch him disappear, then share another smile.

"Well done," says Don. "It's great news."

"We weren't planning on telling Ollie so soon," explains Gabe, "but he overheard us talking and starting asking questions. It seemed pointless fobbing him off with white lies…"

"And he's sworn to secrecy?"

"Well, we'll see…"

"It must be quite early, you know, for Grace…"

"Yeah, she missed this month. She's been to see the doctor, obviously. She's had two, no, three tests – home kits and by the nurse – it looks to be definite."

"I told you not to give up hope. I told you…"

"You did. Not a word to anyone else, mind, Dad."

"Of course not. It's your secret."

There is a pause. Don is still letting the news sink in, rolling it around like a fine wine on the palate.

"Do you know the sex?"

"Well, actually, Grace *does*. I don't want to know."

"Best way."

"I want it to be a surprise. And I'm not bothered either way.

Two boys? Brother and sister? I'm happy whatever."

Don has become distracted. His eyes wander over to a family photograph on the mantelpiece: the five of them in a group pose in the garden at a party for their thirtieth wedding anniversary. Briefly he is lost in his thoughts.

"I don't want to be pushy," he says presently, turning to face his son. "Not at all. But... but if it's a girl... if it's a girl, you could maybe call her Carole...?"

"We had thought of that, Dad." He smiles. "Or Caroline..."

"Caroline? Yes, that's nice. Caroline. Caroline. So, it *is* a girl?"

"No, I said, I don't know. Honestly. I don't have a clue. We've just had plenty of time to think about names."

"And if it's a boy?"

"If it's a boy, then you'll have someone else to play cricket with, won't you?"

COUNTY HOSPITAL

Gabe has been in again this morning. Grace is fine; worn out but fine. A baby due next spring. I'll be a grandfather for the second time. It's a lovely warm feeling. I remember the day Gabe and Oliver told me that she was expecting. I have no shame in recounting that after they had gone, I sat alone at the kitchen table and sobbed uncontrollably for minutes. It was like a dam had burst open.

Everything is becoming much clearer recently. My thoughts have gradually become more ordered, less random. They are keeping me in a little longer for observation of my brain patterns and checks on my blood pressure, but mainly to give more time for my broken bones to heal. My memory of events is, I think, more reliable. Over recent days the police have spoken to me at some length to follow up what I had given them in writing. Ed Coppinger came in too, although it's not strictly his case. Full of the joys. And a personal guarantee that they'd nail the bastard who put me here, a line I'd heard somewhere before.

He also had the sketch of a sorry tale to tell me, news that so far hadn't been made widely public, at least not in Britain: my neighbour Gaynor Otterbridge had been assaulted in Spain by a man she had been staying with on holiday. He was a British national, Coppinger told me under his breath, living near Alicante, whom she had met, apparently, on the internet and who had invited her over for a week in the sun. The word was that she had managed to escape from his apartment but was claiming to the Spanish police that her host had twice attempted to rape her. In the process he had broken her nose. The man, as yet unnamed, had already been picked up but had so far denied all charges. I told Ed that she had mentioned to me some weeks ago that she was planning to travel abroad with a friend. *No, she was there alone*, he replied. *Quite alone.*

My own story is almost at an end, but I am still struggling to remember the day my attacker struck. And there are still a few more elements I need to include. Not just for the investigation; the police already have everything I could give them, and plenty more besides. No, I am writing this for my own sake now. By this stage this has become less an act of record than one of cleansing.

Gabe left me yesterday's local paper. He pointed out a short news item about my case. The police have arrested a man described as a thirty-year-old and local. No more details were released, but Gabe had been told, in private, that he is a builder and his name is Shaun Cuff. I didn't need any further details; no personal description, no photo... I knew him. Shaun Cuff. It was crystal clear. He was the man who, according to Geena Dale, had been known simply as Sharky ever since he stepped into the playground on his very first day at primary school.

SEVENTEEN

The scene plays in the half-empty car park of a large supermarket in the middle of the morning. Don Percey is lumbering towards his car carrying two bags of groceries when, quite suddenly, he is accosted by a thick-set man he immdiately recognises as Sharky. He is striding between cars towards Don, ready to block his path; he lifts off his sunglasses to fix him with an aggressive stare before speaking:

"Oi! Mr Bus driver! Oi, I want a word with you!"

Don is forced to stop in his tracks:

"What? Oh, it's you! You want a word with me? What about?"

"What about? You know exactly what the fuck about!"

"Do I?" asks Don, taken aback.

"Don't fuck about, Mr Bus driver. I know about you. I've been watchin' you. I know where you've been."

"Where I've been?"

"Where you've been. You an' Geena. You fucker. I'm gonna kill you, you big fuck!"

Don steps back apace:

"Whoah! Slow down! What the hell are you on about? Calm down, Sharky…"

"Don't you call me Sharky. My mates call me Sharky, not you."

"So what do *I* call you?"

"You call me nothin'. Nothin' at all. An' you don't tell me to calm down. You fuckin' stay away from Geena, yeah? An' you stay away from me."

"That's a bit difficult, isn't it, Sharky?" asks Don, regaining some composure. "I pick her son up every day for school and the chances are she'll be there to wave him off…"

"So you quit your job, Mr Bus driver. Go an' find another bus to drive."

"I don't think so."

"I'm tellin' you to quit your fuckin' job!"

"Look," says Don, taking a deep breath, "Polo leaves school in a week's time. That's all, just one week. In September he won't even *be* on the bus any more. So relax."

Sharky is rowing back a little but sounds undeterred:

"You stay well away from Geena. You listenin'?"

"I'm listening."

"I know where you live, Mr Bus driver. I know who you work for an' I know what car you drive. I even know where your grandkid lives…"

He looks down at Don's shopping bags and laughs to himself:

"I even know what kind of cereal you eat for breakfast."

"Then you might also know I was in the police force for thirty odd years. I know how to deal with threats and harassment, and…"

"You won't be in a state to deal with a fuckin' pack of cards… You stay away from her. Or you'll regret ever sittin' in that crappy bus of yours." He steps closer to Don. "You need to know that I can be a nasty bastard and I've got a fuckin' evil temper on me. Don't poke me, Mr Bus driver. You'll find I don't make empty threats."

The pair exchange hard stares as if each is examining a fake banknote. Before Don can speak there is suddenly a change in Sharky's tone:

"Jesus, you're an *old* fuck, aren't you? You need a hand with your shoppin'? I don't want you to drop those eggs…"

"Look," says Don, trying to pass by him, "I think you've said enough."

Sharky has already put his sunglasses back on and is now turning away:

"You might be right, Mr Bus driver. An' believe it all. Every fuckin' word I've said."

COUNTY HOSPITAL

As I have lived and worked in the area my entire life it surprises me that when I shop in the town's largest and most popular supermarket, I often see so few people I recognise. Very occasionally it's the opposite and I cannot move for friends, former colleagues, neighbours or just familiar faces who want to stop me in the aisles to pass the time of day. With the sort whom I'd met in a *professional capacity*, there were those villains who scowled and blanked me, those who deliberately avoided me and those who would grab me like an old comrade, shake me by the hand and talk of old times as though we'd been *playing* at cops and robbers in the good old days and now the game was over; there was an edgy respect between adversaries like at the end of a heated sports contest where after all the intimidation, the sledging, the fouls and the abuse, opposing players would embrace at the final whistle and all was forgiven.

It was on a morning like that that I was ambushed by Geena's boyfriend, not long after the time he had made such a performance of interrupting the washing down of his motorbike to show me the latest addition to his wardrobe. His wasn't the first face I knew. I met Frau Clipperton in the queue at the fish counter: I remember she wished me *gute Reise* for my upcoming trip to the Rheinland-Pfalz. She also wanted to mention that Otterbridge & Banks had failed to turn up to give a quote for the central heating system she was having installed in the second of the cottages of her *Doppelhaus*. As I had suggested the name of my neighbour in the first place, a misguided attempt to do him a favour, I felt that I had let her down personally. She would hear nothing of my apologies and cheerfully reported that a different company, employing Czechs and Slovaks, she said, were due to make a start the following week.

From a distance I spotted Beverley Bayley's mother, Harry's wife, with what looked like a grandchild in a buggy; the woman had aged considerably since I last saw her and she was dressed in shabby clothes which were too young for her. I believe she noticed me and perhaps because of that she shuffled away in the opposite direction. So we didn't speak; I dare say neither of us would have really wanted to in any case. I could have asked her if Bev had ever managed to get her life back together but I had no inclination to chase after her. The last time she spoke to me at her husband's trial was less than edifying.

I also bumped into Rita, which was odd inasmuch as I had never seen her anywhere else before other than as a passenger on my bus. She was choosing a bottle of wine and actually asked for my advice as she said she was all at sea trying to understand the labels. She introduced me to her husband who had been pushing around the trolley a pace or two behind her in near silence. He was smaller than I had imagined, had an untidy grey beard and I have already forgotten his name. Colin, maybe.

At the checkout I found myself behind one of the young teachers at Carole's old school; one of the last members of staff she appointed, I think. She was on maternity leave, she said, although her shape made an explanation unnecessary, to be honest. *Twins*, she added, patting her belly and grimacing in anticipation of double the labour pain.

And so, this was how it was, one after the other. And finally, quite unexpectedly, the boyfriend, whose intrusion into my daydreaming was not a pleasant experience. Actually, as he walked angrily away from me, I was just as annoyed with myself as I was with him. Frankly I was at my least assertive when Sharky approached me with a barrage of threats in the supermarket car park. Firstly I had never seen him anywhere other than The Pavilions and the incongruity of seeing him there in town momentarily threw me. Secondly

I was heading to my car carrying two heavy bags of shopping (flowered eco-design, *Save the Planet*), so I probably looked less hunter-gatherer, more surrogate housewife. If I remember rightly, I held on to them as if for ballast throughout our short, distasteful conversation.

It was a busy enough scene, mid-morning, but if anybody else did hear us then they chose to react as though we were discussing the weather; that is to say, people paid us no attention in spite of the raised voices. Provocatively perhaps, Sharky was wearing that leather jacket along with his shades which he took off so he could try to pierce me with his thin, icy-blue stare. He was angry, he was dead serious, he was almost foaming at the mouth. He was so close to my face at one point that I could smell yesterday's tobacco and see the stains it had left on his teeth. But through it all he *was* in control. It was quite a performance, and one which, in spite of my familiarity with his type and their take-no-prisoners testostero-bluster, did have an unsettling effect.

As he strode off purposefully across the car park, I wondered if it had been a chance meeting or if he had actually been following me. Did he really know my address as he claimed? As far as I knew, Geena didn't. And had he been bluffing or had she in fact told him about our meetings? Had she given him the details of the money after all, the full extent of the huge investment I had promised to make in her and her family? *Money for sex, sex for money.* Had that thought stoked the fire of jealousy? And sparked a thirst for revenge?

I stood there watching him walk away between the rows of cars. I was suddenly aware that I was sweating and finally put down the bags. My arms were aching. But he didn't disappear. He didn't walk on, straight out of the car park and into the streets as I expected. Nor did he hop onto a conveniently stationed Kawasaki dirt bike. Instead he stopped and slipped into a vehicle parked about fifty yards from where I was still standing. It was a smoky-blue 4x4, waxed clean, a Jimny, 08 plates. Then as he pulled out to turn away towards the exit, he waved back to me through the open window in a sarcastic mock salute.

EIGHTEEN

The scene plays inside Don Percey's minibus travelling in slow traffic on the edge of town. Under leaden skies he is driving through heavy summer rain on his way to pick up Rita for the start of the afternoon run. The sound of his phone ringing cuts through the steady growl of the engine and the swiping of the windscreen wipers. There is a lay-by up ahead and he pulls the bus over to answer the call. It is Pattermore:

"Don, you there? It's John."

"Oh, hi, John."

"You okay to talk?"

"Yeah, I've stopped. What's up?"

"Listen, is your bus okay for fuel?"

"It's about a quarter full. I'll need to fill her up on Monday for the last few days of term…"

"Right. Okay, it's just that we've got a job on Sunday, last minute as usual, and we're going to need your vehicle. Can you do me a favour and fill her this afternoon on your way back to the yard?"

"Yeah, that's not a problem."

"Thanks, Don. It'll save me a job."

"Okay…"

"Take care. Have a good weekend."

"Thanks. You too."

He ends the call. Is it a problem? Don is wondering. No, not really. Although it will make him later getting back home than he wanted. And it would have to be a Friday, wouldn't it? There's always such a bloody long queue at the petrol station on a Friday evening. Especially in July.

COUNTY HOSPITAL

The bus depot is nothing more than a disused farm yard which the absentee landowner has rented to Pattermore for the past ten years or so. It is at one of the neglected edges of a vast estate which, people said, stretched down, in one shape or another, almost as far as the coast. These days, though, farming it all is too costly. There are tracts of land like it all across the county: corners of fields left to nature untamed, buildings and fences and paved lanes rotting and cracking, waiting for someone to remember they are there, waiting to be rescued one day.

Now I can remember the outline of the dark structures as I turned off the quiet lane and rumbled on to the farm track. There were several derelict barns with broken tiles, empty but for some ancient tractor parts and decrepit machinery. The old milking shed gaped open, its gates long removed, its stalls grimy and abandoned, its roof a skeletal frame of rusting beams. Further along stood a pair of neglected silo bins, flanked by a large mound of worn-out tyres. The hard-standing areas for parking were scattered with puddles and weeds. As for the depot itself there was no diesel reserve, no maintenance facility, just a standpipe by a low broken wall of breeze block for hosing down the buses and a small, secured outhouse which held buckets and brushes, a hose reel, liquid soap, anti-freeze, engine oil and the like.

It was early evening in late July, the rain had stopped, but the clouds were dirty and sullen and my side lights had been on all afternoon. I was back much later than normal. As I swung my vehicle into the yard, the neat row of six coaches lined up ahead confirmed that, as usual, I was the last bus back and I would have to squeeze mine into the only space left in the far corner. Tucked on to a low ledge by the pile of rubber was Pattermore's off-roader: a muddy, battered old Land Rover with two flat tyres. It had been sitting there, lame and useless, for a fortnight. Strands of torn, grey plastic sheeting hanging loosely from the sagging plywood partitions that they once protected suddenly rippled and snapped like ribbons as an angry gust of wind set them flapping. I guided the bus beyond the coaches and reversed into my space in a steady, practised manoeuvre. I cut the lights, turned off the engine, and spent half a minute copying the mileage from the odometer on to my daily chart. I remember I could hardly see to write in the gloom. Grabbing the keys, I opened the door and cursed as I stepped down into a brown pool of water that had gathered by the bin wall.

The figure sprang from behind the silo with such speed and directness that I saw only a blurred black shape in the corner of my eye before the pain of a savage horizontal blow to my shins took my breath away. My legs buckled from the impact and as I landed with outstretched arms towards the feet of the attacker, he stepped nimbly aside and prepared another assault with what looked like a length of steel piping. From behind came a series of heavy strikes to my ribs, hard and fast, cracking bone after bone, a controlled rhythm of beats, metal on flesh, metal on flesh.

A pause.

Gasping for air.

Grunting.

A faint smell of alcohol, then of sweat, lost at once in fading exhaust gas.

I was rocking in agony, holding my broken chest, groaning, my legs throbbing, heart pounding, pulses thumping inside my head. I tasted muddy water, then the salt-flint of blood. I could barely twist my neck to see him, to tell when and if another punishment would come. I could hear him too panting for breath, a scraping of boots through the grit and mud behind my back as he regained his balance. Then a sharp intake of air, and next, before I could picture the downward thrust of his weapon towards my head, or even hear its impact on my skull, a searing axe-head of pain brought a blinding dazzle of light, then a long, lonely free fall into the emptiness of the deepest, darkest pit.

EPILOGUE

COUNTY HOSPITAL, DURNOVER WING

Late September

"You won't be leaving that photo behind, will you, Dad?"

"No. No, I haven't forgotten it."

Don Percey is shuffling around the edge of the bed on a pair of crutches. On the wooden bedside cabinet, perched next to a neat pile of get-well-soon cards, is the family photograph: one of the first things he saw when he woke from his deep, troubled sleep several weeks ago. The room is quite bare today. For the past two weeks he has had a bed in the large communal ward, but today he is back, just for the morning; for him it has become a kind of private waiting room. His son Gabriel has helped him pack a bag of items he's had brought in from home, plus the little gifts from visitors, and at this moment the younger man is struggling with the zip. Don looks again at the photo and sighs. He still cannot believe that Carole won't be at home waiting for him with a mug of tea, a Danish pastry and a hug. He reaches over and picks it up with the cards, handing them to Gabe.

"Here, put them in a side pocket somewhere, would you?"

The day has come at last when Don is allowed to leave the hospital, and this room for the last time: his womb, his life-support, his refuge, his ivory tower. He feels like a convict must feel at the prospect of release. The day has come when he can start to live his life again, free, refreshed, reborn into the outside world. But Don is unsure. He recognises the signs of unease: the adrenalin, the quickening pulse, the nagging doubts. He has already admitted to himself that he has a touch of stage fright.

"By the way," says Gabe, "your neighbour's back."

"My neighbour? Who do you mean?"

"The woman who was attacked in Spain. Mrs Otterbridge, isn't it?"

"Gaynor?"

"Yeah, her. She's back in the country, anyway. Must be a relief. When I was over at your place yesterday afternoon I spotted her in their back garden. Looked like she was having a drink, sitting out in the sun. A youngish bloke with her, dark curly hair."

"That'd be her son. How did she look?"

"Okay, I suppose. Sitting up, drinking, talking. I couldn't really her face properly. Anyway at least she's back safe. I'm sure she's glad to be back home."

"Well, yes and no."

"Yes and no? What do you mean?"

"Well, between you and me, I don't think she has the happiest of marriages."

"Oh."

"It's just an impression."

"Oh."

"They don't seem to do much, you know, together, as a couple."

"Well, not everyone can have thirty years of wedded bliss, Dad. Not everyone is as lucky as you."

Lucky? Don is shocked that his son can use the term to describe a marriage that was abruptly ended by a tragic accident, the most awful stroke of misfortune. Had he already forgotten the fallen scaffolding, his mother's suffering? Of course he hadn't. Don needed to lighten up. Gabe hadn't meant anything by it but he has read his father's expression and he regrets his choice of words.

"Sorry, that came out wrong," he says. "I meant lucky that you have so many happy memories of Mum."

"I know what you meant, Gabe. It's alright. You're right, anyway. Up to a point. We *were* lucky, I suppose."

Don is wondering how much, if anything, his son knows about Graeme Robledo-Brown. If he has read Don's record, his long and fragmented statement, then he will know plenty. But in all these recent days Gabe has said nothing about the man, nothing about his relationship with Carole, *his compadre, his good companion, his treasure.* The detectives had told Don that his recollections would remain confidential, that their circulation would stay strictly within the parameters of the investigation. If this meant that Gabe had not had sight of the documents, then the police had for once been as good as their word. One day Don might be of a mind to show Robledo's letter to his son, but the chances were that he never would. Nothing good could ever come of it.

Gabe grabs the holdall and lifts it off the bed.

"Right then, if you're ready, old man, I'll take this out to the car."

"Where are you parked? You know I can't walk far..."

"Yes, of course, I know. Dad, relax. The nurse will bring you a wheelchair and I'm going to move the car round to one of the ambulance bays. They said it'd be okay there just for a few minutes while we get you on your way."

"So I'll wait here?"

"Well, you're not going to chase after me down the hall, are you?"

Gabe smiles at his father. He is still not quite the man he was before. Don has been dressed in a check shirt and a thick woollen sweater; a bit heavy for the day - it's muggy and still outside - but better to be on the safe side. A pair of sloppy shorts were the easiest things to get over his legs, both still in plaster at the shin. There's a blanket to cover his knees later. Gabe looks again at his father's face, pale and drawn. In two months he has lost a lot of weight.

"So, I'll wait here."

"Yes."

Don sits down on the bed and rests the crutches against it, but they both fall to the floor with a clatter.

"Don't worry, Dad. Leave them there."

Gabe pats his father's shoulder and carries the bag to the door. Just as he steps out into the corridor, he turns back.

"Dad, by the way. You have a visitor here. Your last one, I suppose. She's been waiting outside. I'll tell her to come in."

Curious, Don looks up from his thoughts to see a familiar figure appear in the doorway, then step cautiously into the room. Geena Dale is smiling at him self-consciously.

"Hello, Don."

He stares at her as he might a mirage, then edges forward to stand.

"No," she says softly. "Don't get up for me."

She has a sun tan and today her hair is bleached blonde: a little longer than he remembered, and it looks like she's been to a proper stylist. She is wearing a loose white tee-shirt (with *Babe* in sparkly lettering), pink stretch jeans and scuffed black high heels. Her perfume is new, lighter, expensive. A neatly drawn tattoo in the design of a Celtic knot decorates an elbow. She is carrying a cloth shoulder bag. Ever the detective, Don has noticed all these fine details.

"How are you feeling?" she asks. "It's good to see you."

It takes a moment for the situation to become real to Don. He has spent weeks writing about this woman. From addled memory he has studied her from all angles, heard her voice again from sassy catcalls to timid whispers, seen her both forceful and vulnerable, witnessed moments of anger and of tenderness. He has been touched by her smiles and her tears, moved by her spirit. In those months in which her hair has changed from red to pink to black to sandy brown and finally to peroxide, she has amused him, beguiled him, entranced him. He focuses again on her, her actuality, her presence, the woman here in the hospital room, standing slightly nervously in front of him. And then he is thinking: she really does have a great figure.

"Geena. What a nice surprise."

He hasn't seen her since the morning of the Friday he was attacked; he had remembered only a few days ago that it was Angelo who had met Polo off the bus that afternoon. Her hair has grown, but he cannot calculate exactly how long ago that was. He's been told, of course, but dates and times are still hazy. He knows that she hasn't visited him here before, but he doesn't blame her for keeping away.

Geena closes the door and moves slowly into the room. Don may be out of bed, dressed and ready for release, but to her he still looks like a patient, washed-out, grey hair razor-cut, grey face thinner than she remembers.

"I'm sorry I've not been to see you before, Don."

"That's okay."

His throat is suddenly quite dry and his voice sounds brittle to his own ear. He looks over to the bedside table for a glass of water but there isn't one.

"Sit down," he rasps. "Bring that chair over."

She lifts the plastic-backed chair and parks it opposite the bed, close to Don. She sits and calmly takes his hand in hers.

"Don, I couldn't come. You understand that."

Her eyes are lowered, she is pinching an earlobe between her thumb and forefinger.

He covers his mouth to cloak a short cough.

"Really, it's okay."

"You know I'm so sorry for what happened to you, yeah?"

Then, looking up at him,

"You believe me, don't you?"

Don returns her look.

"Geena. I believe you are sorry. Of course, I believe you. I don't blame you."

"Thanks..."

"But *what exactly* are you sorry for, Geena?"

"What do you mean?"

"Have the police spoken to you?"

"Yeah, course they have. They know all about you and me. An' your money an' your promises."

"I told them," Don cuts in. "I had to. They made me write what you might call a personal witness statement. So it's not a secret anymore, but it doesn't change anything…"

"Course it does! It changes everythin', Don. It does for me, anyway."

"How?"

"Listen, I can't stay here long. I've spoke to your son. I rang him last week. I told him I needed to see you one last time."

"One last time?"

"Then I told him I'd be gone. Gone for good. He was very kind. He's the same kind eyes as you, Don. He said I could see you today, just as you're leavin'."

"What do you mean, gone for good? One last time?"

Don has pulled his hand away.

"Don, be realistic. You're not going to be drivin' Polo to my house anymore. You've no reason to come. Have you? Where were you really thinkin' this would all end?"

"Is this coming from Sharky? Has he told you to say all this?"

"No. It's me. Sharky don't tell me what to say. Anyway, he's done one. Pissed off. He's left."

"What do you mean? He's done a runner? Isn't he on police bail?"

"Bail? No, he's free, Don. He's innocent. *He* didn't attack you."

"He didn't?"

Her cheap cotton bag is on her knees now. She fidgets with the hemp loop which holds it closed over a fat wooden button.

"I don't suppose I can light up in here, can I?"

The question is fatuous, more to herself. Don ignores it.

"Are you saying it wasn't Sharky at the bus yard?

"No, it wasn't. The police had him in and out, in and out, but they can't pin this on him. He hated you, Don, but he didn't try to kill you."

She is suddenly tired of holding the bag and drops it to the floor at her feet.

"He was with me that evenin'. We were off out together. He's bought a little jeep. We were drivin' around. We ended up at the seaside."

"So you're his alibi?"

"Yeah. I was. I am."

"Were there other witnesses? There, *at the seaside*?

"Listen, Don. We've had all the police stuff. I'm sick of it. They've had me in too. More than once. Bullyin' me. Insultin' me. You know what they're like. Pricks. It's the truth, anyway, so there's nothin' else. We were together until it went dark. Don't start asking me all those fuckin' questions again, Don. I've answered them all. An' I told the truth. I did. We both did. Even if they didn't believe us they had to believe the CCTV when they finally got round to lookin' for it. We were filmed buyin' a takeaway, thank God."

The detective Don once was has nowhere further to go with this.

"Sharky did not attack you," she goes on. "He's gone, he's buggered off, but that's got nothin' to do with you. That's between us. Me an' him, yeah? But I swear, Don, he did not attack you."

Don looks away from her to the window. Through the open blinds he sees a patch of grass, a small tree with browning leaves and the flat bricks on an adjacent building. He knows this view better than any other. He has seen geraniums bud and bloom pink and apricot and crimson, seen them fade and drop; he has watched the pale green leaves of the maple sparkle and flutter, seen them deepen and burnish and glow orange in the evening sun. There is not the lightest breeze today. It has started to rain: a soft, ghostly drizzle.

He turns his face back to the woman who has her hands to her mouth. Her eyes are closed.

"So who did?" he stabs. "Who did attack me? Do the police know this yet? Are they any closer?"

Geena draws breath, and stares into his eyes.

"They're nowhere. They're clueless."

She hesitates. He is listening, waiting for more, like a beggar with a bowl.

"Geena. Tell me. Tell me what you know."

She waits, then sighs.

"I'll tell you. I *came* to tell you. You have a right to know. I get that."

"Then tell me."

Another moment's pause. She composes herself and lowers her voice.

"It was Mal."

"Mal? Malcolm?"

"Yeah."

There is a blank moment as the name sinks into his consciousness, like a pebble tossed into a pond.

And then Ashworth is there in front of him, lolling in his deckchair, in his sweat-stained Batman tee-shirt, the prince of the Pavilions, father when it suits him. He gives him a wink, takes a deep swig from a can of lager and raises it towards him in an unsmiling, ironic gesture of respect.

"Wasn't he in London? I thought he'd…"

"No. He came back. About a week before. You know what I'm like with him. Soft as shit."

You look strong, Geena, but you're not, Don is thinking. You're as fragile as a sparrow chick.

She smiles defensively at her own frailty, then goes on:

"He found out about you. About us. Not the money. Just the meetin' in the pub that time. Someone who knows him saw us together in the pub. An' he saw the new stuff I'd bought in the house, Polo's bike, the telly, new clothes, an' he put it all together in his head - he jumped to a conclusion. Shit, he went mental…"

"So why didn't you tell this to the police?"

"Christ, I can't shop him, Don…"

"He could have killed me, Geena! He *tried* to kill me!"

"No, no, he swore it was just a warnin', just a beatin'…"

"A warning? *Just* a warning? So would you have shopped him if I had died? If he'd actually finished the job properly and finished me off?" "

Geena is not answering. She is looking at her knees.

"Geena?"

"Look, I can't be sendin' him to prison, Don. I can't." Her voice has trailed off to a whisper. "He'd be shut up for a long, long time. He's already on a suspended sentence…"

"What the hell is stopping you? He hits you, he steals from you…"

"He's Polo's dad, Don," suddenly louder.

"When he can be bothered…"

"He's Polo's dad, and Amber's. He's their dad. I can't send their dad to jail. Polo needs him."

"Needs him? He doesn't need that bastard around."

"He needs a father, Don. I think I know my kids better than you do, for all your good intentions."

Don is stung and needs a moment to recover.

"So what's to stop *me* telling the police exactly what you've just admitted to me?"

"They've already had him in. Twice. An' Angelo. Angelo is in the clear, he was at home, drinkin' with next door, an' Mal's got an alibi too."

"An alibi? You said he was in the bus yard beating the crap out of me..."

"You heard me say it, but I only said it that once, for you. I'll never be sayin' it again, Don. Do you understand? I'll deny it. Malcolm's got his alibi. He was miles from the bus yard."

"You said you were with *Sharky*...

"I was."

"Well?"

No answer.

"Well?"

"Polo's his alibi."

"Polo? You made Polo lie for you? For him?"

"He was down by the river fishin' with his son."

Don looks at her, puzzled, exasperated, then gasps in disbelief.

"Fishing? That's not even a credible lie!"

The affection he has felt for this woman and her touching vulnerability is curdling quickly into contempt, her weakness betraying his faith like a worm inside a shiny red apple. He drives on:

"I need to see Polo. I need to see him."

"You keep the hell away from him, Don. I mean it."

"You asked a boy, a child, to protect a scumbag like that...?"

Geena stands up, flustered.

"Don't say anymore! Don't you dare..."

"The police won't believe it. A prosecution lawyer would rip him apart in seconds."

"But they *do* believe it. Polo backed him up. He did. He told the gavvers he was with his dad."

"A court wouldn't accept that…"

"Do you really want to put him through that, an eleven-year-old?"

"You're asking *me?* Do *you* want him to go through it? *You* asked him to lie, you or Malcolm, didn't you? How did you manage that, eh? Did you bribe him with some empty promises? Or was it emotional blackmail? That usually works on children."

"If you care about the boy, Don, if you really care about Polo, you'll let it go. You survived. I'm sorry you got hurt, but you survived, yeah? We all move on. Let it go."

Don is lost for words. Anger has tired him. Geena gives him a pained, earnest look, desperation in her eyes.

"Please."

He looks away in disgust.

Geena has edged her chair away from the bedside. She picks up her cloth bag from where it has fallen.

"I'm goin'. I've told you what I came to tell you and that's all there is to say. You can't see Polo. You can't force him to choose between you an' his father. He won't choose you, Don, believe me. He won't. He needs a father, an' for all your money, you're not that and you never can be."

Don tries to get up off the bed, but his crutches are on the floor and he hasn't the strength. Nor has he the strength to fight back. Geena takes another deep breath, drawing the line. Then she opens the bag, takes out a flat beige envelope and offers it to him.

"An' before I go, here's your money."

Don takes it from her, confused, opens it and looks inside.

"There's a few hundred pounds left," she explains. "From the money you gave me. The cheque. I'm sorry there's not more. I *am* grateful. You gave us a help up when I needed it. A big help up. I tried to get Sharky to pay me back what he spent on the jeep but he told me to sing for it. He only knew about the first ten thousand, believe me. When I cashed it, he found it and 'borrowed' half, said it was his share..."

"And what about the rest?"

"The rest?"

"The *tens* of thousands I wanted, I want, to give you and the kids, in the future..."

"Forget it, Don. Please, you've got to put it out of your head. I've cancelled the deal. I can't accept it. No, it's finished."

She is searching for eye contact but his head is down, he is fingering the notes distractedly.

"Where was it goin' to end for you, Don? It's a dead end, honestly. Polo needs a real father, not... not a fairy godfather. Spend it on your own family, yeah? We're okay. We are. You want me to change, but I can't."

He looks up at her.

"I won't change, Don. It's too late for that. I don't *want* to

211

change. I'm me and I get by. In my own way. I'm sorry you got hurt, and I know you meant well."

She wants him to say something, to challenge her, but he has no words.

"You're a lovely man, Don, but I told you not to get mixed up with me. I did, didn't I? You remember? I warned you."

She rubs the bud of a tear back into her eye. Just as Don is about to speak, the door is abruptly knocked open and the nurse Juliet pushes a wheelchair into the room.

"Oh, Don, I'm sorry. I didn't realise you had a visitor. I saw Gabe go off down the corridor, and I thought..."

"Don't worry," sniffs Geena, with a thin smile. "I was just goin'. We've finished."

Before Don can contradict her, the nurse is between them, setting the black tubular wheelchair up against the bed.

"Dr Pickering is on the ward," she is reporting. "He wants to see you before you go. Just to say goodbye, I think, Don, and wish you luck. The rain has stopped. It looks as though it's brightening up for you."

She hasn't noticed the crutches on the floor and runs over one of them with a wheel. Instinctively Don leans to pick it up and immediately regrets his action; his ribs are healed but still sore.

"Oh, thanks, Don. I'd have got that for you."

In the seconds it has taken for Don to look down, stretch, wince, stretch a little further, grab the end of the crutch and pass it to the nurse, Geena Dale has disappeared. Through the open doorway he stares into the passage: flickering shadows are cast on a blank wall by a strip light blinking on and off, on and off.

"Geena..." He mouths her name but his voice fails him.

Back in the room her empty chair is askew, the pale brown envelope lies on the bed sheet like a stain, as the slick, soft clip-clop of her heels receding down the corridor fades to silence behind the distant swing-doors.

AUTHOR'S NOTE

The final text of *Bailing Out* has taken over four years in its stop-start formation. I naively thought I had completed it in February 2012 and it was shortly after that date that I submitted it to a long list of literary agents for consideration. Two things went against it: I had written it in an unorthodox part-narrative / part-screenplay format which jarred with certain readers and at 37,000 words it was too short to seriously interest publishers, being a novella rather than a novel.

In the meantime the story had been filed away, superseded by other projects, revisited and cast aside again. In the autumn of 2015 I picked it up once more, as I recognised after the local success of *Shillingstone Station* that I had another half-decent Dorset story up my sleeve. This time my reworking was more focused. I standardised the prose, making it more readable in the process, sprinkled in a few more characters for colour and texture, developed existing ones, fleshed out the detail of the storyline and revised the dialogue.

Apart from the Dorset setting, *Bailing Out* has little in common with *Shillingstone Station*. True, there is a slow-burning element of mystery. True, it is a novel about human frailty. Even the setting though is less than obvious in this story. Much of the material for the book, the characterisation, the locations and so on, was loosely based on real people and places I was determined not to identify. I renamed, exaggerated and disguised personalities, and I blurred scenes by cloaking them in anonymity. I cannot overstate the fact that *Bailing Out* is a work of fiction. I considered inventing names for towns and villages but believed it to be both disrespectful and dangerous to tread in Thomas Hardy's footsteps, a fictitious Wessex already in existence since the early 19th century. So my landscape is deliberately vague, that of a county recognisable as being in the South West of England, the only real places mentioned outside London (Poland, India, Singapore, Wales and Spain notwithstanding!) being the A303 trunk road and the historical landmark of Corfe Castle.

One other overlap with *Shillingstone Station* is the invaluable team of supporters whom I wish to thank once again, namely my wife Heather for her critical eye, my brother Warren for his attention to detail in the editing process and Honeybee Books for their expertise in the area of self-publishing. Additionally I am grateful for the assistance I received in matters legal from Tom Wilson and in matters medical from Rachel Wood and Gail Bennett. The "someone clever" mentioned in chapter 11 is the journalist and commentator Owen Jones, author of the brilliantly provocative bestseller *The Establishment*.

The idea of telling the story through Don's recollections, both reimagined and then reported, came to me early on in its creation. It allowed me to fluctuate between a third-person narrative and a first-person reaction to that narrative, offering a counterpoint between the reader's view of events and then the immediacy of Don's own perspective. An alternative would have been to tell the whole story from the point of view of a third party, with or without a narrator. However, if the story had been told at one remove, I would have lost the impact of Don's insight when he is at his most raw, at his most vulnerable, reacting to his *addled memory* in a hospital bed with an open laptop at his fingertips.

Geena would have been an interesting but impractical narrator; her lack of education would have made for either an unrealistic or a strangled prose style. Gabe could have provided a clear, articulate but incomplete account. The only other character I seriously considered as my storyteller was Rita. She had the insight, the interest in people, the skills to tell the tale, but fatally not all of the knowledge; Don's confidences to her were given only up to a point. Nevertheless, to offer evidence of her pivotal position between Don and Geena, I have included on my website www.brentshore. co.uk the transcript of part of her interview with the police, conducted shortly after her return from holiday in Majorca.

Brent Shore
August 2016

ABOUT THE AUTHOR

Brent Shore grew up in Hyde, a small town on the eastern edges of Manchester. He studied Modern Languages at the University of Nottingham, where he also trained as a teacher. His career took him firstly to North Yorkshire, then to Bermuda, and finally to the middle of Dorset where he has lived since 1991.

Since retiring from the classroom, he now channels much energy into writing fiction. Following *Shillingstone Station*, which was well received locally, *Bailing Out* is his second novel to be published.

Visit: www.brentshore.co.uk

Contact: stories@brentshore.co.uk

SHILLINGSTONE STATION :
A NOVEL

Andris Fleet's life has been damned by self doubt and insecurity, ever since he was left lame by a mother who had no inclination to care for him and fatherless by a conspiracy to murder in the interests of national security. As his mother admits: *Little Andris, poor lamb, he was born into a cesspool of deceit.*

Aged thirty-five and having made something of his life in the hospitality industry, he chances to find evidence that throws everything he has been told about his father's death into doubt.

A further twenty-five years later and another clue from the distant past emerges which sets him on a definitive search for the truth.

The link between the years of 1960 at the time of the Cold War, 1990 as the Soviet Union falls apart, and contemporary 2015 is the changing face of a small rural railway station in the village of Shillingstone, North Dorset.

Less of a spy story than one of the *generational consequences* of a spy story, *Shillingstone Station* gives the reader a mystery to solve, the coat-tails of a blighted biography to hang on to, and in the end a very human tale of resilience, warmth and forgiveness.

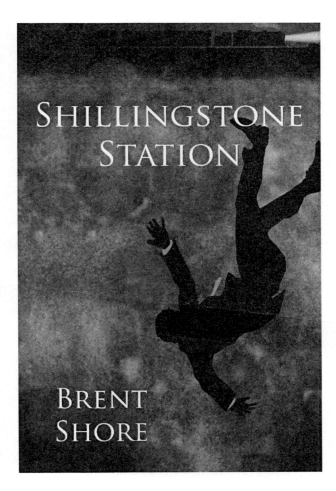

NOW AVAILABLE ON AMAZON